Bury The Bodies

Detective Solomon Gray, Volume 4

Keith Nixon

Published by Gladius Press, 2019.

One

Eleven Years Ago

Detective Constable Mike Fowler leaned on the horn to warn the car in front he was coming. Two minutes ago, he'd been hammering along the London-bound side of the A299 dual carriageway, a wide, brightly lit stretch, and freshly gritted on this wintery December night. His was the fastest vehicle on the highway.

However, Clapham Hill, leading to Canterbury, was a different prospect. He'd taken the Whitstable exit ramp at speed but been forced to lift his foot off the accelerator when he entered the narrow and twisty road. As Fowler shot past a slow-moving Fiesta the driver turned to glare. But Fowler only caught a glimpse of a white face as he overtook, his attention fully on the tarmac ahead.

The road names round here – Bogshole Lane, Fox's Cross Road, Honey Hill – reflected the fact this was in the sticks; lowland rural areas reclaimed from the marsh and sea over the years.

Yet again Fowler made the call to Jeremy Templeton, willing him to pick up. Yet again the call immediately dropped to voicemail. Yet again Fowler disconnected, swore and pressed the accelerator harder.

Soon his headlights illuminated the sign he wanted: Rough Common. He swung a right, his rear wheel catching a patch of black ice. He fought to correct the spin like he'd been trained on the police advanced driving course, losing some speed in the process. Then his tyres gripped and he was on a straight line again. A few hundred yards further was another turn between a couple of houses, both dappled with cheery Christmas tree lights. He headed straight on, along a track, dark and crowded with trees. This was Blean Woods, a relatively small remnant of what had once been a huge forest.

He switched to full beam, pushing back the shadows. The car lurched down as a front wheel hit a pothole. Fowler almost banged his head on the steering wheel. Then up over a speed bump – the exhaust scraping in a metallic screech. He weaved around the peaks and troughs in the track, accompanied by the staccato rattle of grit and stones on the undercarriage. Up ahead was a car park – normally packed during the day, but now empty except for a single vehicle. Fowler slewed to a halt, his lights still on.

He stepped out of the car's warmth into the sudden bite of winter cold. He ran to the other car and glanced inside. Front – his rapid breath fogging the glass – then back. Empty, other than a mobile on the driver's seat. He pulled out his phone, thumbed redial. The mobile in the car rang, the screen bright. Fowler groaned as he disconnected. No wonder his calls had gone unanswered.

"Templeton!" shouted Fowler. Then once more. Nobody besides Templeton would hear him. There weren't houses within half a mile, the woods surprisingly isolated. It was the perfect spot to bury a body. Fowler wondered how many more Templeton had entombed here. Templeton was a 'cleaner', he made people's problems go away. But not this one – it couldn't happen. Fowler shivered, the sharp wind cutting deep.

He ran back to his car and turned off the engine, killing the headlights. He shrugged on a jacket and grabbed a torch from the glove compartment, his mind attempting to work out where Templeton would go. Fowler turned on the torch, but the bulb didn't illuminate. He slapped the torch once, twice. The bulb flickered and finally lit.

Fowler considered his options. Several paths stretched around and through the woods – short, medium or long depending upon your preference. Circuits which began and ended here. Templeton wouldn't want to go far, not carrying the dead weight of a corpse, in case he bumped into a rambler. Dogs were more of a concern because they had keen noses and a tendency to dig. So Templeton would bury the body deep.

Fowler took the right-hand path. This was where walkers usually emerged – the end of the circuitous journey. Where they would be focused on getting back to the car and going home. Where children would be tired. The torch's narrow beam lit a small circle of ground beneath. Fowler willed the batteries to keep going. Bushes and trees crowded him, their bare branches knocking against one another in a gust of wind.

"Templeton!"

Fowler kept moving until he saw a pale brightness ahead, off in the verdure. He paused, cocked an ear and listened: whistling – tuneless and shrill. Fowler stepped off the firm terrain onto soft undergrowth, rotting leaves and thriving moss. He pushed at the branches and boughs of saplings and bushes to make his way through. His trousers snagged on something. He heard a tear. The torch beam showed a long, snaking bramble. Fowler lifted his leg high over the obstruction, causing the fabric to rip some more. He swore but got moving again.

As he forged on, the whistling grew louder, and the brightness increased. He found Templeton in a small clearing beneath a pine tree, its boughs shrouding the small man like the wings on a devil. Templeton was cutting a hole, building a pile of dirt. A torch perched in a tree branch cast enough light for Templeton to work under.

"Templeton," said Fowler.

The man whirled around, the spade raised up to his shoulder, clutched in both hands, ready to strike. His mouth was open, his eyes wide. A second later Templeton recognised Fowler, let the shovel blade drop and leaned on the handle.

"Bloody hell, Mike," said Templeton, "you scared the crap out of me! This place already gives me the creeps." He pushed long dark hair out of his face. Templeton was an ageing rocker and had the hairstyle to go with it.

"Where's the boy?" Fowler stepped forward, grabbed Templeton by the arm. "Where?"

A frown creased Templeton's face, seemingly puzzled that Fowler would ask. "In the boot of my car."

"How is he?"

"Fine. He's just drugged." Templeton's frown deepened. "I don't kill people, just put them in the ground and let nature take its course." He shrugged off Fowler's grip, took a step back so he was out of reach.

"Why the whistling?"

"To keep back the ghosts, of course."

Fowler sagged. The relief made his gut churn. He'd been convinced Tom Gray was dead. "There's been a change of plan. Go back to the car and wait for me."

"What change? Why?"

"He's to be taken back to Margate for a few hours before somebody else picks him up?"

"Who?"

"You don't need to know, believe me." Fowler held his hand out for the spade, which Templeton passed over. "Take this." Fowler offered Templeton his torch. "Go and wait for me."

Templeton appeared ready to fire more questions at Fowler, but he shook his head instead, grabbed the torch and left. Fowler took a few moments to calm, before shovelling the damp loam back into the hole, all the while knowing how close it had come to being a silent grave for a child. When it was filled, Fowler stamped the mound down then spread some pine needles over the top. Within a few days the earth would appear untouched.

He stretched up for Templeton's torch and made his way back to the car park – faster than his outgoing trip. He shone the beam into Templeton's car. Templeton was in the driver seat, waiting, engine running. Templeton blinked in the sudden bright light. He wound down his window.

"Can you get that out my face?" asked Templeton. Fowler shone the beam at the ground. "So, what's the new plan?"

"Do you know the Sunset Guest House?" said Fowler.

"On Fort Road?"

"That's the one."

"Take the boy there. Someone will meet you."

"You've got to be kidding me, Mike. It's right by the police station."

"I'm well aware of that."

"What if somebody sees me?"

"Just make sure they don't."

"I'm not happy about this."

"You'll be fine."

Templeton shook his head. "This wasn't what I agreed to."

"It is now."

"No. It's too risky."

"You have to."

"You take him." Templeton opened his door and made to get out. Fowler blocked Templeton's path. Pushed him back into his seat, grabbed him by the throat. Templeton thrashed, trying to lever off Fowler's grip but Fowler was strong. Templeton hit Fowler's arm until he let go.

"For fuck's sake, Mike!" croaked Templeton, rubbing at his neck. If looks could kill.

"You're wasting time. I've got to go back to the station. I'm already exposed by being out here when I've no reason to be."

"Not my problem."

"One call and I'll make it your problem. You owe us, remember?"

Templeton glared. Fowler let him think, mull over his situation. But not for long.

"I do this and we're square, right?" said Templeton eventually.

"If we're in the clear, you're in the clear."

"All right." Templeton was a fool if he thought mere words made everything okay. He pulled his door closed, started the engine and drove off.

Once the sound of Templeton's car had died away, Fowler took off his coat and got inside his own vehicle. The interior was like a fridge. He twisted the ignition key, set the heaters blowing on full before he picked up his mobile and made the call. It was answered immediately.

"I made it in time," said Fowler.

"Thank God for that!" Fowler heard his boss, Sergeant Jeff Carslake, blow a huge sigh of relief. "Well done. Get your backside here soon as you can, we need to talk about what's next, but not over the phone."

"I'll have to change my trousers first."

"Why?"

"I tore them on a bramble. They're shredded."

"Jesus, Mike. There isn't time for this crap. Just move your arse." Carslake disconnected.

The light from the mobile died, leaving Fowler in near blackness, the trees above him blocking out the glow of the city and most of the stars. He remembered how he'd got here, saving the life of his friend's son, but condemning him to owing a debt to the wrong kind of people. Just a few hours ago, he and Carslake had interviewed Solomon Gray, talking over the moment when Gray had realised his son was gone. And, all along, Carslake had the answer.

Fowler cursed the day he'd arrived at the scene of Valerie Usher's murder, when he'd been sucked in and couldn't escape whole. But there was no going back now.

Two

Two Weeks Ago

Acting Detective Inspector Solomon Gray wasn't one for stakeouts. They weren't his thing, including the unauthorised ones. Not because he didn't have the patience. Quite the opposite. The problem was, he was a people watcher. Passers-by were interesting; distracting. It was often the curse of the more introverted, like himself – he preferred observing people to interacting with them. And on the busy streets of London there were always plenty to side-tracked by.

This was Gray's third trip to the capital in two weeks. He always took the train. Driving meant leaving a trail, and Gray wanted anonymity. He'd have to pay the congestion charge to enter central London and the NPR system – number plate recognition – would log his journeys in and out. Plus, as the adverts used to state, he could let the train take the strain.

He stepped out of the carriage and passed through the ticket barrier before heading towards the sign for the London Underground – a red circle with a horizontal line through the centre.

Gray descended two flights of escalators. The smell of the underground hit his nostrils. He tried to define the pungent odour. A combination of grease and earth mixed with the metallic tang of ozone. However, Gray reckoned if he asked ten people to describe the aroma he'd get ten different definitions, and in multiple languages.

The escalator mechanism clacked beneath his feet. Gray stood to the right, leaving the left free for the speed merchants to charge down the steps. In front and behind, people were on their phones – talking, messaging, listening to music. For a place with so many people it was utterly impersonal.

Once at the bottom, Gray headed for the Northern Line, the black route on the underground map. He waited on the platform, an overhead digital sign telling him the next train was under a minute away. A wind preceded the train's arrival, the gust picking at his coat. Brakes screeched until the train halted, and only when the doors opened did his fellow travellers remove their attention from their phones to step inside before returning to what they'd been doing previously. There were warning beeps, then the doors closed and the old metal carriage shunted forwards with a jerk. Gray already had hold of a handrail in preparation. The train knocked along the bore of the oldest underground train system in the world.

Just one stop east and Gray was reversing the process, out onto the platform, up an escalator, away from the smell and into the light once more. His journey had been short, and he was still in central London, zone one. This was Angel, Islington. Property here was expensive, even for the capital. Busy with tourists and traffic, where wealth butted up against poverty. It pained Gray to shake his head as he passed an imploring beggar, but he couldn't save them all.

He could taste diesel fumes in the air. At a steady pace it took Gray ten minutes to reach the narrow opening of Rawstone Street. Strictly he was in Finsbury now, not that you'd be able to tell from any boundary signs – there were none.

Gray was here for Lewis Strang. The name given to Gray by Jeremy Templeton. A connection to his missing son, Tom. Gray had found Strang quickly enough, but then hit a wall. Because Strang was a cop. A detective inspector in the Metropolitan Police. Effectively a colleague and out of bounds. But not when it came to Tom. Gray simply had to move with more caution. Getting a home address had been straightforward. And Gray had learned more about Strang via local publications like the *London Evening Standard*. DI Strang was high profile, a prolific detective with a penchant for finding his way into the press and onto the TV.

So Gray knew what Strang looked like and where he lived. And the latter was what gave Gray additional cause for caution. A detective inspector shouldn't be able to afford a three-bedroom mews house with off-street parking unless he'd come into money via the lottery or an inheritance. The rent on a similar property, just a few doors along from Strang's, was in excess of five grand per month.

During Gray's previous journeys here he'd spent his time scoping out the CCTV, shops and bars where people congregated, the quiet spots where nobody went. But this would be his first walk past Strang's house. Gray sauntered along, pretending to enjoy the sights along the route, openly staring at each of the residences. He paused near number 26, Strang's, to tie his shoelace. The ground floor was a pair of garage doors, flush with the pavement; a front door braced by two olive trees in massive ceramic pots, too heavy to run off with; then two storeys of windows above. Nothing remarkable. Gray stood.

"Morning, Sol."

Gray turned, surprised to see Detective Inspector Marcus Pennance beside him. Gray hadn't heard his arrival. Pennance was a handsome, well-dressed, and well-groomed man. He looked mid-thirties, but was actually early forties. He looked after himself, went to the gym and drank the required daily amount of mineral water. Pennance was the picture of a modern single man.

"Marcus, I didn't know you lived around here."

"You should have told me you were coming. We could have got together."

"Last minute decision," lied Gray. "I'm in between meetings."

"Like the previous Thursday and the Sunday before?"

Gray was unable to keep the surprise off his face, whereas Pennance was, as usual, impassive as a rock.

"Come on," said Pennance. "I'll buy you a coffee. Then we can talk." Pennance turned and got walking, not bothering to check if Gray was following which, of course, he was. He had no choice if he wanted to know what the hell was going on.

Pennance led Gray to a nearby café which was part of a big chain. If Gray were honest (which he usually was) he preferred independent places. Gray found the coffee on the mild side. His partiality was towards bitter. He wondered what that said about him.

"Grab a seat," said Pennance. "I'll order."

Gray picked a crumb- and sugar-laden table by the window; floor-to-ceiling plate-glass separating inside from outside. Using a napkin, Gray scuffed the worst of the detritus onto the floor, as it appeared previous occupants had too. He sat down, watched people hurry by, oblivious to his stare. All the while he wondered why Pennance was here. Maybe their objective were the same.

A minute later, Pennance arrived with a tray; a large cappuccino for himself, double espresso for Gray. There were two sealed paper drinks cups too.

"What are you doing, Sol?"

"Taking in the sights."

"I can think of better attractions. The Houses of Parliament, Tower of London maybe. Or the British Museum? A West End show? But not a row of houses."

"I'd heard a Banksy had been painted on one overnight."

Pennance actually laughed. "That's a good one. Very clever. I didn't have you down as an appreciator of urban art."

"There's a lot you don't know about me, Marcus."

Pennance raised his coffee in a salute. "We can all say that, my friend. So, what's your interest in Lewis Strang?"

The surprises kept coming. Gray took a moment to think, stalling by sinking half the espresso.

"Who?"

Pennance shook his head, disappointment evident. "Don't mess me around, Sol. I'm not an idiot."

Gray knew Pennance was right. He had a sharp brain. Gray decided to come clean. "It's about Tom, of course."

"Ah." Pennance sat back. "How?"

"Strang's name came up recently. I'm following the lead. And if we're being so honest with each other, why are you here?"

"I'm part of an undercover surveillance operation on our mutual friend. We've been keeping an eye on him for a while.

You were beginning to stray a little too close this morning to where we were located. I used the excuse that I was getting us all a coffee before you were spotted." Which explained the two takeaway cups. "I'm trying to do you a favour, Sol. The last thing you want, I'm sure, is to come to the attention of the Met. People would start asking what your interest is."

"Have you moved departments?"

"I'm still with the Sapphire Division." The Metropolitan Police unit's primary concern was child exploitation. "I need you to stay away from Strang; let my investigation run its course. I can't have you blundering around. If we bring him in I'll get what you want from him."

"If?"

"Nothing's guaranteed in life, you know that."

Gray drained the last of his espresso, slowly, carefully put the cup down. Another avenue blocked, like so many over the years. But there were ways around every obstacle. He wouldn't give up.

"I've never steered you wrong before," said Pennance. Which was true.

"Don't make me regret it."

"I will if you come back."

"Train fares are bloody expensive anyway."

Pennance grinned, picked up the takeaway cups. "Thanks, Sol." Then he was gone.

Gray bought another coffee and wondered what to do with his time now.

Three

Now
Gray turned his car into Union Row, a narrow line of terraced houses off the main road on the corner of the College Square shopping centre, which ran along the Margate seafront. He paused; a strip of blue and white tape stretched across the road, flapping in the wind, blocked his access. Somebody behind Gray beeped their horn, unhappy at their rush-hour progress being hindered. The car swung past. A frown, a shake of the head. A bad start to their day, but worse for the murdered man Gray was waiting to see.

The uniform managing the perimeter, a young constable Gray recognised but didn't know, glanced through the windscreen, before unhitching the tape, allowing Gray access. Gray wound down his window. "Where's good to park?"

A quick glance up the street. "Behind the Iceland van, I'd say, sir."

"Thanks."

Gray drove on, the cobbles of this old street of working men's residences bumping beneath his wheels. Gray spotted the gap the uniform meant; tight really. He took a few goes to back in. When he'd achieved this minor miracle of geometry he walked further along Union Row – the spring sun starting to warm the day – until he reached the locus, delineated by more tape, this time yellow and stating, "Crime Scene Do Not Pass".

Beyond the tape, a line of four uniforms, each spaced an arm's length apart, were slowly walking away from him, heads down. Their eyes would be focused on the road surface below, in a search for potential clues. A handful of crime scene investigators, wearing white protective suits and blue overshoes, milled about the immediate area. One, squatting down over what looked to be a carrier bag, lifted a camera and snapped a photograph, then another from a different angle. A sequence of small yellow cones crossed Union Row, connecting the carrier bag to the corpse.

A few yards along was Pump Lane, which joined Union Row to Union Crescent, running adjacent to the Al-Birr Community Centre and Mosque. On the opposite corners of Pump Lane was the Union Surgery (a general practitioners') and the Union Church which was of Methodist denomination.

The entrance to Pump Lane was blocked off too, meaning nobody could get in or out of the immediate area without Gray's permission. He was now senior investigating officer and the scene was his.

Hands in pockets, Gray caught the attention of Detective Constable Jerry Worthington, one of the station's new recruits, recently transferred from his home town of Newcastle. Worthington's rugby player bulk stood out, despite the shapeless evidence suit. Worthington, hood down and mask dangling around his throat revealing a V-shaped soul patch underneath his lower lip, nodded at Gray and walked over, gait self-confident.

"Morning, sir." Worthington yawned. "No need for the gimp gear, we're pretty much done." Worthington lifted the tape for Gray who bent at the waist and entered the crime scene. "He's over here."

Worthington led Gray to the corpse sprawled on the pavement, randomly spotted with pale circles of chewing gum. This was College Walk, a narrow alley which joined Union Row to the usually busy shopping centre.

A young black man lay prostrate just beyond the three bollards which marked the alley entrance. Gray paused a couple of feet away from the body and adjacent to a dried stream of blood which had pooled around the corpse and run away in a narrow flow; evidence the man had bled out. Scattered about the carcass was the debris of the unsuccessful attempts by paramedics to revive him. The discarded wrapper from a syringe, gauze, dressings. Despite valiant efforts, the man had died on this dirty strip of tarmac.

Gray tilted his head, took in the black tracksuit with double white stripe running down the arm and leg, the unzipped top revealing blood-soaked white T-shirt, the youthful face with open eyes which stared into nothingness. He was wearing a baseball cap, a large NY logo in the centre.

"How old would you say he is?" asked Gray.

"Late teens to very early twenties." Which was what Gray had thought. "Expensive pair of trainers for a kid."

"I'll take your word for it." Nikes. Gray knew the distinctive tick logo but he had no idea about their value beyond the brand name. "I don't recognise him."

"Me neither."

Thanet was a relatively small place, broadly comprising the three conjoined and sprawling towns of Margate, Broadstairs and Ramsgate which curved along the easterly finger of the Kent coast and pushed into the English Channel, the busiest shipping lane in the world. The cops were aware of the repeat offenders; the thieves, the nonces, the druggies.

"Boughton will for sure," said Worthington.

"Good point. Get him over, let's have a chat."

Worthington left Gray and interrupted the nearest of the uniforms carrying out the fingertip search. A moment later, the uniform was talking into the Airwave radio attached at his shoulder before he nodded and Worthington returned. "Boughton's on his way."

PC Damian Boughton arrived a minute later from the direction of Pump Lane. He was a local man, walked the same beat for most of his career, Union Row and the surrounding streets was on his patch. Greying, balding, he wore a short-sleeved shirt which revealed faded tattoos. Boughton was like the station's extreme weather vane. If he wore a coat then it was very cold and everyone should wrap up tight.

"Morning sir," said Boughton to Gray. He nodded at Worthington. "I understand you want a word about the victim."

"Have you seen him before?" asked Gray.

"No, sir, not at all. I've a very good memory for faces. And I've been asking around, talking to the kids. So far he's a stranger."

"Carry on constable."

"Yes, sir." Boughton retreated.

"Clough's been and gone," said Worthington once Boughton was walking away. Clough was the Thanet pathologist, a thin and wiry man with a penchant for pedantic detail.

"What were his initial impressions?"

"That the kid was dead." Worthington grinned. Gray did not. Worthington had a tendency towards laddish humour which grated on Gray. Worthington picked up on Gray's displeasure and replaced the smile with stoicism. At least he wasn't stupid. "Multiple stab wounds to the torso and one to the leg, probably a cut artery. See all the blood around him? It pumped out fast. He didn't really have a chance."

Knife crime was one of the fastest rising issues in the country and Thanet was no exception. It was a vicious circle whereby kids carried weapons to feel safe, but statistically those who did so were the ones most likely to be victims of violence.

Gray glanced over the body. One of the trouser pockets was inside out, some loose change beside him. Gray pulled on a pair of nitrile gloves before patting the corpse down. He found a set of house keys in the other pocket, but nothing else. "You didn't come across a phone nearby? Or wallet?"

"Neither."

"I'm assuming he wasn't attacked here?"

"Definitely not, sir." Worthington led Gray back across to Pump Lane, following the line of small individually numbered yellow cones. Beside each was a blood splat. Worthington stopped by the carrier bag Gray had seen photographed earlier. "This is where he was likely first assaulted, dropping his bag in the process. Given the spacing between the spatters, he ran from his attacker and collapsed where we found him." A good hundred yards between the two locations. "He made a 999 call from where he lay."

But the paramedics were too late. Gray shifted his attention to the carrier bag; it was from the supermarket, Morrisons. There was one on College Square. Gray squatted down. Beside the bag was a glove. It was a standard woven woollen article, thin. The kind supplied in volume to bargain stores all over the country. Gray had a similar pair himself. The victim hadn't been wearing gloves. "Have we found the other one?"

"No."

"I want a DNA analysis on the interior."

"It could have been dropped by anyone, sir."

"I'm aware of that." Gray shouldn't need to tell Worthington that at this stage of an investigation it was about ruling evidence in, not out.

Gray then parted the plastic. Inside was a microwaveable lasagne and a four-pack of beer, the metal dented. Beneath the cans was a pack of laxatives. Remarkably, there was a receipt too. Gray checked the time printed at the bottom.

"When did the 999 come in?"

"10.39pm."

The receipt said 10.35pm. Gray slid the paper into a clear plastic evidence bag. He straightened up, peeled the gloves off.

"So, the victim had in all likelihood gone to Morrisons, bought his dinner and had been returning to his destination, possibly home, given the house keys in his pocket, when he was stabbed."

"I would think so, sir."

"We'll need a search of the gardens and drains within a quarter-mile radius, see if the weapon disposed was of," said Gray.

"I'll get that sorted, sir."

"Have you been to Morrisons yet?"

"On the to-do list."

"Okay, I'll go and check out any CCTV footage."

Typically, pedestrians used the alley as a shortcut to the shopping centre and Gray would do so himself under normal circumstances. Instead he walked the long way around, back to the main road. The constable released the tape barrier for Gray, replacing it when he was through. Gray entered the shopping centre. He was very familiar with the surroundings; it was the nearest large store to the station for a cheap sandwich.

As he went inside, a heater blew a stream of air onto his head, ruffling his hair. Within the store, life went on as usual. Customers came and went with baskets and trolleys loaded with food when, only a few yards away and a few hours ago, a murder had been committed. The fruit and vegetable aisle opened up to one side. In front were tills, and on the other side was a customer-service kiosk.

A harassed woman, bleached hair tied up into a rough bun and wearing a worn green uniform, was managing the counter. A short queue of people waited less than patiently for either lottery tickets or cigarettes. At the front, an old man, a shopping trolley beside him, was trying to return an item.

Gray leaned on the work top, interrupting the transaction. The female staff member turned bloodshot eyes on him; by her expression, less than impressed with his imposition. Gray showed his warrant card.

"Where can I find the manager?" he asked.

"I'll call him for you." She picked up a phone, tapped in a couple of numbers. "There's a policeman down here." She paused, listened. "I've no idea what he wants." Another pause. "Okay." She replaced the handset. "Murray is on his way down."

"Thanks."

She nodded, returned her attention to the queue, sighing when she realised it had lengthened in the interim.

A few minutes later, an efficient-looking man strode purposefully towards Gray across the shop floor. He looked too young, then again, with the long hours and seven-days-a-week opening required in retail, it was an industry for the youthful. Murray's hair was swept over his crown in a wet-look wave, presumably held in place by copious amounts of gel. He wore thick-rimmed glasses, a cheap white shirt (with a sauce stain on the front), pressed black trousers and a green tie bearing the company logo.

"I'm Murray," he said, speaking fast. Like his colleague, he didn't make it clear if Murray was his first or surname. "I hope this isn't going to take long. I've rather a lot to be getting on with." He gave Gray's hand a single shake.

Gray introduced himself. "There's been a murder," he said.

"I know," replied Murray, cutting him off. "It's all everybody's talking about. How can I help?" Murray's eyes flitted around the immediate area, perhaps looking for a shoplifter to tackle.

"He was carrying one of your plastic bags. He was in here immediately before he was attacked."

"Okay, we've got in-store CCTV. Got to monitor everywhere. For thieves, stuff just walks out the door here all the time. I've a target to meet."

"I'd like to review the CCTV footage, Mr Murray."

"Just Murray is fine. No problem, follow me."

Murray led Gray back the way he'd come. He paused at a door set into the wall at the far end of the store, pushed it open and allowed Gray through first. Gray found himself in a narrow hallway, the scuffed magnolia walls of a corridor stretching away to a set of stairs.

"Up here. Excuse me," said Murray and pushed his way past. At the top of the first flight, Murray turned left into the first doorway. It was a small room filled with TV monitors.

"What time?" asked Murray. Gray showed him the receipt. "See this number here?" Murray pointed to a three-digit code beside the time and date. "That's the till identifier. He went through self-service."

Murray sat down, placed his hands on the controls and began winding back through the footage. On one of the monitors Gray watched people reverse in a quick, jerky motion, the clock in the bottom corner of the screen rolling back too. Murray brought the speed back to normal at 10.33pm. There was a bank of self-service tills. Only one was occupied.

"That's him," said Gray. The man's clothes were obvious, even in black and white. He walked up to a till, passing beneath the camera, holding the food and drink. The baseball cap was pulled down low over his eyes.

The man scanned his stuff and shoved it into a bag. When it was time to pay, the soon-to-be victim unzipped his tracksuit top, reached inside, pulled out a wedge of notes, unpeeled one and fed it into the machine. The rest returned to his pocket. He grabbed the change the machine spat out, took the receipt and walked away.

"He didn't pay for the carrier bag," said Murray.

Gray ignored him. "Can you follow him through the store?"

Murray nodded, switched cameras and went through the same motions of rewinding time. From this angle, the man could be seen in the entrance. He pulled a mobile from his pocket and spoke briefly before returning the phone to his tracksuit trouser pocket. He left the store, walking towards his death.

"Thank you, Murray," said Gray. "I'll send a constable round to take a copy of the footage."

"No problem. Happy to help. I'll show you out."

Murray walked Gray through the shop once more, gave Gray's hand the same cursory jiggle, turned and returned to his job. Gray contemplated the footage and crime scene as he walked the few yards back. The victim's mobile and cash had been stolen. Perhaps this was a robbery gone wrong. But, from the camera's perspective, nobody else was nearby to see the pile of cash the victim was carrying. The laxative was maybe relevant. This could be a County Lines related incident – drug dealing by gangs who were based outside the area, transporting narcotics in for sale to the locals, and shifting the cash from the sale back to their base. Like an import–export business – but an illegal one.

When Gray reached the alley's mouth the paramedics were loading the body bag into the back of an ambulance. The slamming of the vehicle's doors echoed. The pair climbed inside.

The engine started, and the ambulance rolled past Gray towards the cordon. The driver gave a quick blip of the siren to shift some of the more persistent onlookers out of the way. As soon as the ambulance was gone, the crowd moved to refill the gap.

DC Worthington wasn't in view. Gray expected he was organising the local area search. For now, there was little more Gray could learn here.

Four

Now

Back at the Margate police station on Fort Hill, less than half a mile away from where the killing had taken place, Gray headed for Detective Chief Inspector Yvonne Hamson's office. It was on the first floor and had been Carslake's. Sylvia, Carslake's personal administrator, had resigned shortly after his death. As yet, Hamson hadn't replaced her. Gray doubted she ever would. It wasn't really Hamson's style to have somebody running around after her, taking messages, making drinks. And there was always the drive to save costs in these days of austerity. Gray entered the office after the briefest of knocks.

Hamson was at her desk, concentrating on her computer screen. She glanced up at Gray's entry, the beginnings of a frown on her forehead. "Bloody hell, Sol. How many times have I told you to wait before you come in?"

"Old dog, old tricks. At least I knocked."

The interior was remarkably similar after the change in ownership, Hamson retaining Carslake's minimalist decor with just a few alterations. The window behind Hamson's desk overlooked the North Sea. A lamp on her desk cast a soft hue. The walls were painted a muted blue, which Gray thought lent the room a cold feeling, though the taint of the solvent fumes had finally eased.

"Just wanted to give you a quick update on the Union Row murder, Von."

"Okay." Hamson stood, crossed to the round table pushed into one corner of the office. She took a chair for herself. The table was one of the new additions. Usually Hamson preferred to hold discussions there, rather than remain behind her desk, metaphorically closed off. It was less confrontational, apparently. Gray didn't mind either way, sometimes a bit of conflict was worthwhile.

"A young black male, late teens, early twenties," said Gray. "No identification on him. He'd been stabbed multiple times and bled out on the street. It appears his phone and a large sum of money was stolen. Could be a simple robbery. He was carrying plenty of cash, which he made visible when buying some stuff from Morrison's. However, from the CCTV, the victim was alone when he flashed the cash and he'd also purchased laxative."

"Bloody hell. Maybe he was just constipated?"

"Possibly. But I don't think so."

Hamson asked, "Is it County Lines?"

"Too early to say, Von. But it's possible."

Recently a new tactic in the ongoing illegal supply of Class A drugs (commonly heroin along with crack cocaine and "legal highs" like Spice) had been coming to light, what was being described in the press and police force as County Lines dealing. It was the movement of drugs from an urban hub into rural towns or countryside locations, developing networks across geographical boundaries to access and exploit existing markets.

Competition for business within the major urban centres – London and Liverpool leading the pack with Birmingham,

Manchester too – had become intense over the last couple of years. Prices and profits were down. People had a tendency to look for other prospects if their current venture was under threat. And somebody somewhere had hit upon the idea of spreading their wares beyond their territory. New supply routes were springing up all the time in multiple locations. There were reputed to be 283 County Lines out of London alone, and Gray would bet that what the police knew was just the tip of the iceberg.

Hamson stood and moved over to a map of Thanet she'd pinned on the wall, pins stuck in where County Lines crimes had occurred in the last two months. She tapped Union Row. The space was empty.

"No other offences have occurred there," she said.

Thanet had suffered a huge spike in drug-related issues in recent months: violence, theft with a deadly weapon, and stabbings. There had been a jump in the number of junkies being admitted to hospital as a result of overdoses, directly due to an increased flow of narcotics, often low quality and spiked.

"Maybe it's a new gang?" said Gray.

Hamson shrugged. "Hopefully when we find out some more about him we'll know."

The typical target was deprived areas, where unemployment was higher and earnings lower than average. The locations tended to be coastal. Margate and Ramsgate, along with Clacton in Essex, were perfect examples, although Gray had heard of issues in other, seemingly wealthier regions, like Brighton in Sussex. Another aspect the press had gleefully reported – the gangs' targets were where policing was "less robust" than the cities they currently dealt within. Which irritated Gray immensely. No way did he or his colleagues take a softer approach than other forces. And if this incident was indeed County Lines in nature it was the most serious crime to date.

"Okay, worth giving Yarrow the heads up." Hamson stood. "I'd better get on, Sol. Unless there's anything else?"

"This is enough, isn't it?" said Gray.

Five

Now

The Incident Room was a large, open space dedicated for use during major operations, comprising desks with phones and computers atop, two meeting rooms off to one side and, at the front, a large whiteboard with a sizeable TV screen fixed to the wall nearby.

However, the Incident Room was no longer for Gray or CID's use; it had been commandeered by Detective Chief Inspector Adam Yarrow's Pivot team. Much more attention was being paid to County Lines because crime statistics were moving in the wrong direction. Hard data was difficult to come by, and only now were the regional forces gathering critical information, though statistical accuracy was problematic. The gangs kept themselves and their dealings small, frequent and low key – more challenging to detect.

The outcome was Operation Pivot, a centrally managed and resourced activity by Kent Police, personally endorsed and overseen by the boss himself, Superintendent Bernard Marsh, specifically created to tackle County Lines activity. The Pivot team was assembled under Yarrow, a rising star in the police service.

Margate was chosen as the first port of call for Marsh's flagship effort. Yarrow's people had arrived two months ago and been working with members of Gray's team since to identify the active dealers and as much intelligence about them and their undertakings as possible.

His hand halfway to the door of the Major Incident Room, Gray's mobile rang. It was Dr Ben Clough, the pathologist. "I've just started looking at the corpse from Union Row. There's something you should see. Can you come over?"

"What is it?"

"Best I show you." There was no point Gray doing anything other than agreeing, Clough wouldn't be drawn, and he wouldn't be calling unless it was important.

"About twenty minutes," said Gray. "There's something I've got to do first, okay?"

"I'll be waiting." Clough rang off and Gray put the mobile back into his pocket.

Gray entered the Incident Room, pausing a moment as he glanced around. He spotted Yarrow leaning over a desk, talking to Detective Sergeant Mike Fowler who'd been seconded from CID to Pivot for the interim. With the exception of Emily Wyatt, another temporary appointment to the team but from the department for Child Exploitation and Online Protections (CEOP), everybody else present had parachuted in with Yarrow. In Fowler, Yarrow had gained local knowledge, and Wyatt possessed previous experience of working in Thanet. She also lived not too far away, in Deal, which kept costs down.

Yarrow was a tall man with a shock of white hair, a large nose and a pockmarked face; acne scars from youth in all likelihood. Yarrow's older appearance clashed with the colourful friendship bands he wore on his left wrist, the ends frayed. Gray knew, because he'd asked, that the bands had been made by his daughters. Gray liked the matter-of-fact DCI. He was here to do a job and that's what he was focused upon. There wasn't any politics to dance around and Yarrow attempted to minimise his impact on the day-to-day running of the station.

Gray headed to the desk; saw some grainy video footage being played on Fowler's screen. Another undercover operation by the look of it. Fowler had proved a marvel at gathering intelligence and he was highly adept with the video equipment. His standing had never been higher within the echelons of Kent Police. Gray carried on past the desk and put himself in Yarrow's eyeline.

The DCI glanced up from the monitor. "Morning, Sol."

"Sir." Gray nodded at Fowler. "I'm holding a case review on the stabbing victim shortly, could you join us?"

"If my presence warrants it, of course."

"It may do, sir."

"What about Mike attending? He seems to know every dodgy bastard around here."

Fowler laughed. "Fine with me."

"What time?" asked Yarrow.

"I'm not sure exactly," said Gray. "I've got to head to the mortuary first."

"Just give me half an hour's notice."

"No problem."

Yarrow returned his attention to Fowler's intelligence. Gray left the room and crossed the corridor to the Detectives' Office. DC Worthington was just taking off his jacket to hang over the back of his chair. Gray made his way over.

"I've got to see Clough; something about the corpse," said Gray.

"Want me to come with you, sir?" Worthington's hand moved towards his coat.

"I'll be okay, thanks. I need you here to get a Murder Board set up."

All the available information from the investigation would be plugged into HOLMES, the Home Office Large Major Enquiry System, now on its second generation. HOLMES was a computer-based investigative tool. A significant enquiry developed a vast number of data points and fast. HOLMES simplified the process of tracking and analysing the information. The system was connected to all the police forces across the UK, so the tools at hand were impressive. But big data was unwieldy data, so the team would centralise on the Murder Board, where the key information such as crime scene photos, an outline of the victim and potential perpetrators was written up.

"Next task, sir," said Worthington.

"And CCTV from the local area? I'd like to review any footage as soon as possible."

"On that too."

"Great, see you shortly."

"I'll valiantly slog away in your absence." Worthington cast a sloppy salute in Gray's approximate direction. Gray shook his head but stayed quiet. He'd done it to Hamson enough over the years after all.

GRAY WENT THROUGH THE process of scrubbing up and putting on a gown, cap, gloves and face mask before following Clough into the Mortuary Examination Room. Gray backed in through large double swing doors. He'd rarely been this side of the operation. The space was bright, well-lit by overhead tungsten lights which cast a clean, bright hue. Everywhere was steel on the horizontal; white tile on the vertical. In the centre of the room was a large drain and the floor was on a slight slope to help with sluicing down. It was like a large, grim wet room.

The dead man lay under a white sheet on a trolley. Clough had removed the clothes and placed them, neatly folded, on a nearby bench. Clough drew back the covering, revealing an already-slit torso. The man's skin had marbled slightly across his chest and shoulders. Gray had seen this effect before; it resulted from the heart stopping. Instead of pumping around the body, the blood was dragged down by gravity to pool along the base of the corpse.

"As usual," said Clough, "I started with an incision down the front of the body, removed the breastbone and opened the ribcage. I removed and weighed the organs. You can see the puncture marks from the knives." Clough touched the skin at several locations on the body. "Long, broad blades. Probably a kitchen utensil. Cheap and easy to get hold of. Sixteen wounds by my count."

"Is this what you brought me here for?"

Clough looked up at Gray. "Of course not, Solomon, but you'll need to get closer to see."

Gray didn't want to, but he stepped forward anyway.

"It was when I reached the stomach that it became interesting," continued Clough. "I left everything in-situ." Clough used his hands to part the stomach cavity. The smell was like that of fresh, raw meat – the slight iron tang of blood – but it was quickly whipped away by the extraction vent positioned beside the torso. There, beneath Clough's fingers, were several plastic bags with a white powder inside. Clough extracted one. He wiped it largely free of fluid and showed it to Gray.

"He'd been packing," said Gray.

"So it seems."

The man had swallowed the bags, more than likely drugs, to transport them from wherever he'd come from. Which explained his purchase of the laxative – to flush himself out. It was an extraordinarily dangerous procedure. Should the wrapping have burst, the kid could have easily overdosed, with potentially fatal consequences. However, it was likely he'd been caught by another significant risk in the drug supply industry – the competition. Poor bastard.

"I thought it best you see for yourself," said Clough. He was right, but Gray never enjoyed the experience. "I've taken his fingerprints. I'm hoping the PNC will spit something out soon." The PNC was the Police National Computer, where crime records were stored. "That's all for now."

"Thanks, Ben. You've given me something to work on," said Gray.

"No problem." Clough picked up the bone saw, a small tool with a circular blade which rotated at very high speed. "I'll let you go before I put this to use."

Gray didn't hang around. He was almost back at his car as his mobile rang. Worthington.

"Sir, we've an address for the victim. Just a few doors away from where his body was found."

"I'm on my way."

WHEN GRAY ARRIVED AT Union Crescent a quarter of an hour later, both cordons remained in place. He parked in almost the same space as earlier in the morning and walked along the street. Worthington and a PC were waiting outside an innocuous terraced house. The front door of peeling green paint led straight inside from the pavement and stood open.

"Found some CCTV footage which pointed roughly to where he lived," said Worthington. "Tried a few doors and showed a photo of the vic and we think we've got the right place."

"Think?"

"The house is divided into three flats, one per storey. Nobody recognised the photo but we were told a junkie lives on the top floor. We knocked but seems nobody's home."

"What about the landlord?"

"No idea who owns the house. There's some company called 123 Lettings on the deeds, however the phone number on their website goes straight through to an answer machine."

"In that case, lead on."

The interior was a plain hallway, stripped dark floorboards and white walls. Worthington hit a large circular button on the wall and a bare lightbulb burned overhead. Worthington took the stairs, passing a door with a brass letter A on the outside. Gray followed, the PC on his heels. They passed flat B just as the light went off, dipping the space into a half-darkness. The PC found another button and pressed it. The trio resumed their climb. Worthington paused on the top flight outside C.

"Try one more time," said Gray.

Worthington hammered on the door with the side of his fist, paused, shouted, "Police, open up!" He bashed the door again. The light clicked off. Gray listened, thought he heard shuffling within. He nodded at Worthington who repeated his banging a third time.

"All right, all right!" A man's voice, Northern Irish accent. After half a minute the door opened an inch and an eye appeared in the gap.

Gray held up his warrant card. "DI Gray, we've some questions about a person who may have been staying with you."

"Nobody here now." The man sounded out of it, his voice slurred and slow.

Worthington put the victim's photograph up to the door. "This man, do you know him?"

"No," he said then pushed the door closed. Worthington, ready for the manoeuvre, dropped his shoulder and stopped the movement in its tracks. "Nobody here now. Go away!"

"This man," said Worthington leaning into the door, "he's been murdered."

The pressure was suddenly released and Worthington spilled forwards a-pace into the flat. A short and stocky man wearing a dressing gown and slippers, his legs bare, stood there. "Dead?" he asked.

"Yes," said Gray. "Just outside."

"Jesus, Mother, Mary and Christ."

"Can we come in?"

The man retreated, turning into the first doorway. Gray followed, entering a living room which smelt of unwashed bodies, decaying food and cat piss. The man dropped into an armchair. Around him were wrappers from fast food outlets, pizza boxes prevalent. A ginger tom immediately leapt into his lap. The man absently stroked the pet.

BURY THE BODIES

"What's your name, sir?" asked Gray.

"O'Rourke."

"Who is your friend?"

"He's not my friend, don't know him, don't know his name, never know any of them."

"What was he doing here then?"

"Gave me some drugs, wouldn't leave."

Gray understood. It meant the flat had been cuckooed.

It was common for dealers to exploit the young or vulnerable to move cash, to store or sell drugs out of a cuckooed property. Typically victims were already users themselves, which O'Rourke appeared to be. Once gang members took over, it tended to be an ongoing cycle of abuse and violence. Which explained O'Rourke's initial reticence to let them enter, but now he knew his unwelcome lodger was dead, the rules of the game had temporarily changed. There was nobody present to manipulate him.

"When did he arrive?" asked Gray.

O'Rourke shrugged, his eyes bleary. "Yesterday maybe?" If O'Rourke had been out of it, the normal passage of time wouldn't have meant much to him.

"Have there been others staying here?"

"On and off."

"How many?"

"I'm not sure. All these black fellas look the same to me." O'Rourke shrugged. "They took my room, the feckers."

"Where is it?"

"Down the way." O'Rourke pointed back out the door but made no move to show them.

"Stay here with him," Gray told the PC.

Worthington followed Gray along the dingy corridor. They passed a bathroom; reached a bedroom. Gray slipped on a pair of gloves before pushing open the door. Inside was a single bed, a wardrobe, a wooden dining chair and drawers. It was relatively neat and tidy.

Gray entered. He pulled open the wardrobe, giving it a hard yank because the door stuck at first. A rucksack was inside. A tug at the drawstring revealed some clothes.

"Sir," said Worthington. He pointed at the drawers. On top was a scrunched-up train ticket, a rectangle of orange and white with black text printed on it.

Gray smoothed out the paper. An off-peak single from London St Pancras, dated yesterday. Which gave Gray a window to evaluate, but the number of people heading through one of the capital's busiest stations in a day would be huge, even midweek. Still, it was something.

"Get CSI over here to give the flat a going over," said Gray.

Worthington pulled out his mobile to make the call but it rang before he could do so. He listened for a few moments and said, "That's great news." Worthington turned to Gray. "We've found a knife."

"Where?"

"On the corner of Addington and Princes Street." Only a few hundred yards away, barely a couple of minutes' walk.

"Ring CSI while we head there."

Back in the living room, Gray said, "DC Worthington and I need to be elsewhere. CSI are on their way. Keep an eye on things until then."

"Yes, sir."

Gray switched his attention to O'Rourke. "One of my colleagues will arrive shortly to take you to the station."

"Why?"

"To interview you about the man who was staying here."

"Will there be tea?"

"I'm sure we can organise some."

O'Rourke raised a calloused thumb.

"Let's go," said Gray. He descended the stairs with Worthington; took a right immediately outside. A few minutes of brisk walking brought them to Addington Street. A street cleaner – its yellow lights flashing – was parked outside the Theatre Royal. A long black tube snaked out from the rear of the vehicle; its neck paused above a drain, the cover removed and put to one side a foot or so away. A man in full-length orange coveralls leaned on the wing, appearing totally uninterested in proceedings.

A PC approached Gray as he neared. "It had been dropped down the drain." The PC held out a clear plastic evidence bag. Inside was a long-bladed kitchen knife. The handle was wrapped with sticking plaster, the kind you purchased as a length and cut strips off as required. There wouldn't be any prints on the handle, the tape wouldn't support them.

"Get it off for analysis," said Gray. Worthington took the bag from the PC. "I'm just going to give Hamson a quick update."

Gray rang her. "Things have moved fast since we last spoke. Clough found the victim was packing drugs, he was staying in a cuckooed property and it looks like the murder weapon has turned up. I think it's safe to say the murder is County Lines related."

"Well at least we know," was all Hamson said.

"I'm going to hold the case review when I get back to the station. There's a lot to discuss."

"I'll attend if I can. Just make sure you invite Yarrow."

"Already done."

"Marsh is going to love this."

There was nothing Gray could say to that.

Six

Now Gray took his place last. Worthington, Yarrow, Fowler and Hamson were already seated around the rectangular table along with three other CID colleagues. A television was mounted on the wall but, for now, the screen was dark. Gray clicked the mouse on the laptop in front of him, waking the display.

"Thanks for coming," said Gray. "For those of you unfamiliar with the case, earlier this morning 999 received a call from a man claiming to have been attacked. Paramedics discovered the victim suffering multiple stab wounds. Unfortunately, efforts to save him proved unsuccessful and he died at the scene. We have a recording of the call."

Gray played the audio file. "Hello, 999 emergency, what service do you need?" asked a woman, her voice tinny through the small speakers.

"Fuck." A man's voice. He sounded shocked. "I've been fucking stabbed."

"Sir? Where are you?"

"I've been stabbed, get me an ambulance! I'm bleeding bad, man."

There was some background noise, rustling, a moan.

"I need to know your location, sir. Can you see a street name?"

"I dunno, man. I'm not from round here."

There came a long, drawn-out groan followed by a dialling tone over which the operator repeatedly shouted, "Sir!"

"The victim's call cut off at this point," said Gray. Nobody else spoke. "This is our man." Gray held up a photograph: the dead man, his eyes closed, taken at the mortuary by Clough and emailed through earlier. "As yet we don't know his identity." Gray slid the image across the table. Yarrow picked it up, stared at it briefly before handing it to Worthington who didn't give the photo a glance before he passed it on. "There are no hits on MisPers of anybody matching his description. Nothing yet on his fingerprints and his DNA is being matched."

"He's a clean skin then," said Yarrow. Somebody without a record, unknown to the police, an increasingly common tactic used by County Lines gangs.

"Possibly." Gray continued, "Prior to the attack, our victim was purchasing food and laxatives from a nearby supermarket. He paid cash, from a large wad of notes, though no money was subsequently found on him. Neither was a phone, yet we know he placed or received a call shortly before the attack. He was wearing expensive trainers, and narcotics were found inside his stomach during the post mortem.

"In the last hour we've received additional information. His base was a cuckooed property only a few yards away from where he was attacked. CSI are on site now."

"What's the address?" asked Yarrow.

"Union Crescent."

"Not one of our target properties," said Fowler. "This is a new one."

"We've taken the resident in for questioning," said Gray, "but he appears to be a user rather than a dealer. We found a train ticket dated yesterday indicating he came from London. There's an enquiry into the Met to track his movements."

Gray clicked the mouse. "We also found a knife." A photo of the weapon next to a standard plastic ruler came up on the TV screen. "Approximately thirteen inches long. Note the taped handle. No fingerprints. We're still awaiting the PM report, but we expect this is what was used on the victim.

"Jerry has tracked down some CCTV which makes interesting viewing." Gray nodded for Worthington to take over, pushing the laptop over to him. Worthington clicked the mouse. The footage appeared on the TV screen.

The recording was in black and white. A single person, hood raised, head down, walking the immediate area in a loop – up the street, turning into Pump Lane before reappearing a few minutes later, completing the circuit.

"Our suspect spent a good ten minutes milling around, heading along Union Crescent, crossing the road and back again," said Worthington. "While the suspect was out of sight, the victim exited his residence and made his way towards the alley, for Morrisons." Worthington paused to let the scene unfold. "Our attacker spotted the victim but chose to lie in wait for his return." The hooded man shifted towards Pump Lane, standing just back from the corner, leaning nonchalantly against a wall, keeping his face turned away from the lens and the victim. "See how he doesn't look directly at the camera? He knows it's there." The scene carried on, a clock in the bottom corner ticking the seconds off.

Worthington wound forward. "This is when the assault occurs." The victim came from the direction of the shopping centre, along the alley. He crossed the road, his rolling gait causing the carrier bag to swing in his grip. As he passed the entrance to Pump Lane, the man pushed off the wall. He must have said something because the victim paused and turned.

As he did so there was the flash of a knife, in and out of the victim's torso, over and over. The carrier bag fell to the pavement. The victim managed to shove his attacker away. The attacker swung the knife once more, catching his quarry in the thigh. The guy staggered away, pulled a phone out of his pocket, placed it to his ear. "That's the 999 call," said Worthington.

His assailant followed in the dying man's footsteps, just a few yards back, shadowing him like a lion stalks a wounded antelope, ready for the coup de grace. He made it to the alley before slumping against a wall, as if he could no longer stand. The killer closed in, grabbed the phone from unresisting fingers, ended the call and put it into his pocket. He raised a hand, in defence or as a plea – impossible to tell. The attacker batted it off and carried on searching, reaching inside the dying man's tracksuit top. "He's taking the money," said Worthington.

The attacker walked away while the victim slowly slipped sideways and lay on the ground.

Worthington paused the video. "A few minutes later the paramedics turn up but they're too late. No witnesses. It was all over quickly. The best we can say is the killer is white and of average height. I can't determine any distinguishing features from this."

Something niggled at Gray. "Go back a few minutes, would you? To when he searches the body." Gray stood up and put himself next to the TV. The scene played over again. As the attacker walked away for the second time, Gray said, "Stop." He tapped the screen. "See there?" A small dark dot on the ground. "I think that's the glove we found."

Worthington squinted. "Are you sure, sir?"

"It's hard to tell, but it's in the right area. Maybe our man dropped it."

"If so," said Yarrow, "any DNA may lead us to whoever did this."

"Get onto the lab, Jerry, and tell them to shift the glove up in priority."

"Yes, sir."

"Does anybody have any further points to make?" There were several shakes of heads. "That's it for now then, we'll keep you appraised of progress."

The meeting broke up.

"Do you need me for anything else?" asked Worthington.

"No, we've plenty on," said Gray. "Good work by the way, Jerry."

"Thank you, sir."

Worthington left but Gray stayed behind for a few minutes, shutting down the laptop, taking a breather. He felt shattered, but also elated. It had been a busy day, but they were picking up pieces of the puzzle.

Back at his desk, Gray read his email. There was a note from Clough, the post-mortem report. Gray scanned over it, picking up on the key phrases. The blade used was long enough to nick the victim's bones at both the front and back of the ribcage. Clough estimated a minimum of twelve inches. Based on the lacerations it wasn't serrated, just like the one found down the drain. Gray now felt certain they had indeed found the murder weapon. Cause of death was blood loss from a slashed artery. Even if the paramedics had arrived immediately, the man would have been very unlikely to survive.

A shadow fell across Gray's screen. It was Hamson, blocking the light. "Have you got a minute?"

"Sure." Gray pushed back his seat.

"Not here." Hamson turned and walked away. Gray followed her outside and into the car park.

She lit a cigarette, standing downwind from Gray. "You're making good progress with the murder investigation. The glove is interesting."

"Time will tell. How did your conversation with Marsh go?"

"Surprisingly, he was fine; even thanked me for keeping him up to date."

"You made the right call then," said Gray. Hamson pinched the bridge of her nose. "Are you all right, Von?"

"Just tired. It seems somebody's always wanting a piece of me."

"When Pivot goes down, you can bask in the glory."

Hamson made a pfft sound. "Marsh will be all over that. Our successes are always his and vice versa."

"Things will quieten once Yarrow is gone."

"And the enquiry is out of the way."

"Yes, I'd forgotten about that." He hadn't. A public examination of Carslake's apparent suicide was due in a few days.

"It'll be fine."

"I hope so."

Hamson's phone rang and she rolled her eyes. "Better get back to it." She took one last drag of her cigarette, dropped the tab to the floor and ground it out before heading inside.

Gray's phone vibrated. A text which said, "Where are you?" With a smile, he replied.

Soon, Emily Wyatt was standing next to him. He yawned, said, "Sorry. Been a tough day."

"No problem, I totally understand. It's been crazy for me too. So, I've got a proposal for you." She theatrically glanced over both shoulders before placing a hand on Gray's chest and leaning in closer to whisper in his ear. "I can't be bothered driving all the way home. How about I stay at your place? As long as you're not too worn out, that is."

Gray grinned. "I think I'll be okay."

Wyatt pecked him on the cheek. "See you later then." And she was gone.

IN THE CAR ON THE WAY home Gray speed-dialled Pennance.

"Sol, hi. To what do I owe this displeasure?"

"I'm on the scrounge for a favour."

"I suspected as much. What specifically?"

"We had a kid murdered here yesterday. He was traced back to London."

"I saw the update from Yarrow. We're co-ordinating cases, remember?"

"Why do you think I called, Marcus?" Gray couldn't keep the exasperation out of his voice. Pennance always had to have an answer.

"Sorry, go on."

"I haven't heard anything yet from your colleagues. I want to know whether he was just transiting through the city or if he was from the area."

"Christ, Sol. Do you know how much footage they'd have to sift through? It's needle-in-a-haystack stuff, mate. If there was a time stamp on the ticket that would help. Three trains an hour head down your way. And that's if he went direct. He could have changed at another station first."

"Why would he?"

"To save money."

"He had plenty of cash on him, a thick wadge from what we saw on CCTV."

"Not his funds though, Sol. All the people who run these operations are tight bastards. Every penny they spend on their runners is a waste as far as they're concerned."

"Can you give them a kick anyway?"

Gray heard Pennance sigh over the car speakers. "I'll try."

GRAY LEANED INTO HIS fridge and pulled out two beers. When he shut the door the kitchen plunged back into darkness. Gray headed out to his balcony. He'd let Wyatt in just a few moments ago. They'd kissed briefly before Wyatt asked for a drink. Gray handed her the beer.

"I still can't get over how good this view is," said Wyatt. She was standing at the railing, facing outwards.

"Are you talking about me or the sea?"

Wyatt laughed. "The sea, of course." It was why Gray had bought the flat, part of a relatively new apartment block right on the cliffs above Louisa Bay in Broadstairs. It took as long to get to the ground floor as it did from the front entrance to the beach. Minutes.

"How's the case going?" asked Wyatt. She turned around, leaned against the railing, cradling the bottle.

Gray sighed. "More questions than answers unfortunately."

"Do you think it's related to Pivot?"

"Yarrow seems to think so." Gray drank some beer. "What's going to happen when the Pivot team moves on?" They were planning a series of raids soon. Once complete, Pivot would relocate to the next problem area.

"I really don't know, Sol. I'm involved because of my child exploitation experience. Sadly it's not an issue unique to Thanet. My best guess is I'll shift over with Yarrow. Probably to Sheerness, from what I hear."

"Pity." Gray liked seeing Wyatt around the office.

"It's not as if we live far away from each other." Deal was about a thirty-minute drive.

"Yes, but our respective workloads will be a challenge."

"It's not that different to now."

"I suppose so." But Gray wasn't convinced.

"There is a bonus, of course."

"What?"

"We can be open about our relationship. Stop all this skulking around."

"That's true." To date, they had managed to keep their private lives totally under wraps. "All those detectives in the office and none of them have figured it out."

Wyatt laughed again. "I've got news for you. Nobody's really that interested in us."

Gray pouted. "And I thought I was the centre of the universe."

Wyatt put the bottle down and closed the gap between the two of them. She placed her arms around Gray and kissed him long and slow. When she pulled away she said, "Right now, you are to me." And she led him inside, closing the French window behind them.

Seven

Now Gray rose early the following morning. He slid out carefully from under the duvet like a bedsheet limbo dancer. The gymnastic exercise was worth it because he managed not to disturb Wyatt. She remained on her back, asleep. Gray grabbed a few clothes from the wardrobe and drawers before he took a shower in the main bathroom, rather than the en-suite, and dressed there too before heading into the station.

He made a coffee in the kitchenette in one corner of the Detectives' Office. The worksurfaces were pristine, all the tins in the right place, no milk left out, because the cleaner had been in overnight. Once his CID colleagues arrived, the area would take on the appearance of a brewing war zone. Back at his desk, Gray activated his mouse and dropped into his email account. He had hundreds of unread messages; mostly they were junk or valueless internal memos. He focused on the new emails at the very top.

Annoyingly there was still nothing from the Met on the victim's movements. Without an identity, Gray was missing a vital chunk of information. However, the lab had pulled out the stops and analysed both the knife and glove.

As anticipated, the knife was free of fingerprints. However, traces of blood had been found on the blade which matched that of the victim. But as a lead on tracking down the killer, the knife was another dead end.

When he turned his attention to the report on the glove, Gray forgot all about the coffee. Trace DNA had been identified inside the fingers. And there was a match to a name in the database. The odds that the match wasn't correct corresponded to one in a billion – high enough for Gray to be sure of the data.

Jason Harwood.

Gray had previous experience of Harwood. He was a low-level fence who specialised in shifting stolen electrical goods. He also did a bit of dealing on the side.

Gray rang Hamson. Judging by the background noise, she was in a car. He told her what they'd found.

"Harwood? That little shit," said Hamson. "How likely is the match?"

"Extremely likely. There's a potential problem, though. He's associated with one of the targets for the upcoming Pivot raids."

"Who?"

"Damian Parker. They're friends." Gray knew because he would be leading the team who'd be arresting Parker in a few days.

"What's your concern, Sol?"

"I don't want to blow the operation."

There was a pause; Hamson would be mulling over Gray's issue. "I can't see it being a problem. Let me deal with Yarrow. I'm sure he'll understand."

"In that case, I'm going to need a search warrant."

"Get the paperwork started. I'll be in as fast as I can to get it signed off."

ONCE THE DOCUMENTATION for the warrant was complete, Gray emailed it to Hamson. As part of Operation Pivot, a huge amount of intelligence had been gathered on local drugs lines. Who sold, who bought. Where trades were carried out, where the players lived. What their circumstances were, what they did with their time. So it was a straightforward process for Gray to pull Harwood's file, which listed his home address, movements, associates and habits.

Harwood was still at the foot of the hierarchy. A twenty-four-year-old lowlife who supplied from a line run by a London-based gang. He operated in Ramsgate, where he lived. Harwood was typically late to bed, early to rise. His dealing was active in the dark hours, in the belief his business was harder to spot. Any electrical goods he sold on occurred in the pubs at night. During the day he fried bacon and burnt toast at his uncle's beachside café, seemingly perfectly legitimately, though Gray wouldn't be surprised if a little bit of powder was shifted alongside the rolls and coffee.

Unsurprisingly, Harwood possessed a record, a litany of petty to medium crimes. From shoplifting to burglary. One count of ABH, for which he'd received a custodial sentence, another of handling stolen goods. But murder? That was a huge leap from his previous form.

Social media presence was sometimes worth checking out too. It was a good way to learn more about the person, as people revealed far too much about themselves on the platforms. So Gray hit the usual apps – Twitter, Instagram, Facebook, Snapchat. He had a number of potential hits on Twitter, but the sometimes convoluted usernames made it difficult to be sure he'd found the actual Harwood he wanted. One candidate appeared likely until Gray realised they lived in New York. Twitter was a bust. There was nothing on Instagram or Snapchat either.

Facebook was the same; lots of people called Harwood. None of the profiles had Harwood's photo; several possessed generic images, such as a car or a dog. Gray went back and clicked on each in turn. He found Harwood on the fourth attempt – a snarling pitbull.

Harwood's timeline was filled with photos of him posing, trying to appear cool and gangster-ish. Gray selected the blandest but still relatively recent photo, one of Harwood half-smiling into the camera, wearing a Boston Red Sox hat beneath a hoodie, and printed off several copies.

Gray returned to the file, moving onto Known Associates. Nobody Gray had experience of, just a handful of equally nondescript low-grade guys. One called Smith, another named Ingham, and a Drinkwater. The team had captured a video of Harwood with his friends. Gray reviewed the recordings briefly, but it told him little other than Harwood was guilty of dealing. Finally, Gray checked the time. The café didn't open until mid-morning, so Harwood should be at home.

His internal extension rang. It was Hamson. "Paperwork's all done, Sol. Go get him."

SIGNED WARRANT IN HAND, Gray arrived at Staner Court, an apartment block which loomed large over the Newington Estate of Ramsgate. Like its nearby neighbour, Arlington House, which dominated central Margate not far from the police station, Staner Court had recently undergone an external assessment following the Grenfell Tower fire in London. Although neither tower possessed external cladding, the residents had long been loudly complaining about the building's general state of repair, or more precisely, the lack of it. Finally, someone in the council had relented and they'd found issues with external render on both constructions. Bits of the outside had been falling off. There was some concern about the balconies too.

Gray was accompanied by Worthington and six PCs, just in case Harwood decided he was going to resist. One positive about making an arrest in an apartment block existed – only a single way in or out of the residence. Just a front door. Harwood could make the leap from of a window, but it would probably end messily.

He stationed two uniforms in the lobby, in case Harwood managed to get past him and downstairs. Then Gray and the rest of the team took the lift to the ninth floor. He placed two further uniforms at either end of the corridor adjacent to Harwood's front door. Worthington stood at Gray's shoulder, the remaining two PCs at his back.

The door opened wide soon after Gray's knock. A young woman wearing a stained grey T-shirt, her hair held up high on her head by a plastic clip, and a baby on her hip, sucking her thumb stood there. A slightly older girl clung to one of her legs.

"DI Gray, DS Worthington," said Gray. "I've a warrant to search your property and for the arrest of Jason Harwood."

"What this time?"

"I'm afraid I can only discuss that with Mr Harwood."

"He's asleep." She moved to allow them access. Gray smiled at the toddler but she carried on nibbling on her nail.

"What's your name please, Miss?"

"It's Jackie Lycett."

Inside, coats and jackets hung on hooks fixed to the wall, a line of shoes and boots just beyond. There were photos of the children, smiling. None of Harwood.

"Jason," shouted Lycett. Receiving no answer, she went deeper into the flat and yelled again. "Jason!"

"What?" A man's voice, half asleep.

"Police. For you."

"What's going on?"

"How the hell would I know? Jesus!" She turned to Gray, jerked a thumb into the bedroom. "He's in there. Sorry, but the little one needs feeding." She walked away, trailed by the girl, seemingly unmoved by her partner's troubles.

Harwood exited the room, tying a dressing gown around him. His hair was tousled, several days of growth on his chin. He rubbed an eye, faded tattoo letters on each finger. "What's all this about?"

Gray showed his warrant card. "We'd like to ask you some questions, Mr Harwood."

"Why?"

"Not here, down the station. Can you get dressed?"

"I haven't done nothing."

"Put some clothes on, please."

"No! Nut until you say why. Jackie, tell them!"

She was in the corridor, standing in the entrance. "Leave me out of it." She backed away, closing the door.

"Christ, Jackie!" Harwood shouted. "Fat lot of help you are!" He reached down, picked up a shoe from the floor and threw it in her direction. It hit the wood with a thud.

"Piss off!" shouted Lycett, muffled. The baby started crying.

"Fucking kid's not even mine."

"Mr Harwood," said Gray, "I'd appreciate your cooperation. It doesn't need to be difficult."

Harwood turned his focus back on Gray. His shoulders sagged.

"All right, give me a minute." Harwood retreated into his bedroom.

"Watch Harwood," Gray told Worthington before he followed in Jackie's footsteps. He knocked on the door.

"What now?" shouted Lycett. Gray entered a living room. "Oh, sorry," she said. "I thought it was him."

"No problem, Miss Lycett," said Gray. "I know these situations can be difficult."

A cartoon was playing on a large flatscreen television, the little girl planted a few feet from it, paying no attention to Gray. Gray didn't recognise the programme. A yellow sponge with limbs and a face cavorting with a starfish. Strange. Lycett was beside an open window, leaning against the wall, smoking. The baby was nearby in a cot, kicking its legs. Jackie must have been lying when she said he needed a feed.

"I need to search the flat," said Gray. "We'll intrude as little as possible."

"Help yourself. I'm used to it." Lycett shrugged. "And I've got these two to worry about."

Gray left Lycett, closing the door behind him. A few moments later Harwood was standing in the corridor, wearing jeans and a hoodie.

"Hands behind your back," said Gray. A PC stepped forward, cuffs in hand.

"Why?"

"Jason Harwood, I'm detaining you for murder. You do not have to say anything, but anything you say may be taken down as evidence and used against you. You have the right to a representation. If you do not have a lawyer one can be provided. Do you understand?"

"No, I fucking don't! Murder?"

"Hands," repeated Gray.

Harwood reluctantly relented, placing his wrists behind his back. The PC ratcheted the cuffs.

"Take him to the kitchen and let's get searching," said Gray.

"What are you looking for?" asked Harwood.

Gray ignored him and began the process of sifting through the family's possessions, starting in Harwood's bedroom, which smelt musty.

It took about a quarter of an hour to find what they wanted. In a box at the back of a cupboard was a single glove which appeared to match the one found on Union Crescent.

Eight

Then
Fowler felt uncomfortable as he waited for Carslake to return from the large wraparound bar. He was pressed into a corner, back to the wall, seated at a circular table. He glanced around, assessing the youthful faces. Their attention was on having a good time, not on a pair of tired men in wrinkled suits.

"Here you go," said Carslake, sliding a pint over, the wet glass leaving a trail like a snail across the damp surface.

"Cheers." Fowler sank half of it in one go, wiped his mouth with the back of his hand, and settled into the seat, feeling not in the slightest bit relaxed.

"Templeton made it."

"Good." Fowler had half-expected Templeton to dump the boy on the roadside and make off, the stakes too high for him. And for everybody else now.

"Everything will be fine."

Fowler twisted his head to stare at Carslake, who'd taken the spot adjacent, rather than opposite. This way they were close to each other, less likely to be overheard. The pub was packed to the rafters with revellers. Music thumped, the bass tugging and pushing at Fowler's chest like an external irregular heartbeat.

Carslake had brought Fowler to the Royal in Ramsgate, a large waterside bar cum club with alcohol and entertainment over two floors. It was always busy and stayed open late. Fowler had driven home straight from the Blean Woods, changed his trousers then headed over here. He'd parked beside the harbour, waiting until Carslake showed. The bouncers had moved to let Carslake past. "He's with me," Carslake said, hiking a thumb at Fowler. No entrance fee applied to either of them.

The interior was bright, a DJ called Sway wearing headphones to one side, on a small stage elevated over everyone's heads, two massive speakers bracing him. The DJ was old-school, mixing on a record deck. No CDs for him. Fowler could see the sense of their location. Everyone was either drunk or trying very hard to be. He and Carslake were just two more people, out for a bad time, anonymous.

"It's not right, Jeff."

Carslake shrugged. "Had to be done."

"Why?"

"Best you don't know."

Fowler snorted. The very words he'd shot at Templeton earlier. "One day you'll have to tell me."

"One day, maybe." Carslake made it sound like that would be far in the future, if ever. Fowler finished his pint, pointed at Carslake's glass. "Not for me," said Carslake, holding up a hand.

At the bar Fowler ordered another. While he waited for the beer to be poured he looked over his shoulder. Carslake was staring at him, seemingly measuring Fowler, maybe assessing his will for what was ahead.

"Three-eighty, mate." The barman pulled Fowler's attention away. Fowler paid, carried the pint back, narrowly avoiding a spillage when a drunk woman bounced into him while she was dancing. She had long brunette curly hair, large dangly earrings and imposing ruby-red lips. She apologised, laid a hand on Fowler's arm and a kiss on his cheek. Then she rubbed at the spot she'd planted her lips before carrying on waving her arms in the air and sashaying her body to the music on unsteady feet. Fowler regained his place and sank another large chunk of his beer.

"Slow down," said Carslake. "Can't have you being done for drunk driving."

"I'm sure I'll be fine." Fowler raised his pint at Carslake. "Friends in high places and all that."

Carslake leaned in, so close Fowler could feel his breath and smell stale garlic. "You need to deal with this, Mike. We've got a job to do."

"He's a kid, our *friend's* kid."

Carslake receded. Fowler noticed Carslake couldn't meet his eye. "Which I'm well aware of." Carslake hadn't said Tom's name since the moment it all started.

"Templeton was going to kill him."

"I stopped that." Carslake's focus was back on Fowler. "As soon as I heard I stepped in. It's created some... difficulties, each of which needs handling."

"By me, you mean."

"By us. We both have a part to play."

Fowler was about to reply, when shouting broke out over to their left. Bouncers moved with sudden speed, pushing their way through the clientele to reach the source of the trouble. The music continued, unabated.

"Keep out of it," said Carslake, unnecessarily. Moments later the bouncers unceremoniously dragged two men, still shouting the odds at each other, to the entrance. Once the door snapped shut the interior returned to its previous state, the pair already forgotten. A new track blared out across the pub, something pacey and heady.

"What do you want?" asked Fowler. He knew he was in too deep to simply walk away, despite being desperate to.

"You're to meet someone."

"Who?"

"Lewis Strang."

"Strang?" Fowler was stunned. The man was a legend in police rank and file, a high-flying copper.

"He's the best at what we need."

"Which is?"

Carslake paused before he said, "Disposal."

"I'm not doing it."

"He's going to put the kid somewhere safe. Not kill him."

"Where?"

"All these bloody questions, Mike." Carslake slapped the table. "Something else not to know. Either of us. When everything's finalised you'll drive the kid to a pre-arranged destination and hand him over. Strang will take it from there."

"No way."

"You have to, Mike. There's no one else I can trust. And besides, the kid likes you." Carslake's words punched a hole in Fowler's soul.

"Oh my God." Fowler sat back, dropped his head on his shoulders and stared at the ceiling, which was a riot of reflected, twirling colours from a disco ball.

"This has to happen. You know it."

"I need more booze."

This time Carslake headed to the bar without uttering a word. Fowler was well aware of Carslake's manipulative nature. Fowler was simply being given time to consider his situation. But Fowler already knew Carslake was right – it *did* have to happen.

"What about the evidence trail?" asked Fowler when Carslake returned. "The Sunset, Templeton's car, Templeton himself."

"The car and the guest house are easy. And Templeton owes me."

"Is that enough to keep him quiet?"

"I'll make sure it is. Which is my commitment in all of this." Carslake checked his watch. "Time to head off, Mike. We've a long day tomorrow."

Fowler shook his head. "I'm staying for a while."

"Thought you might say that." Carslake stood. "Just make sure you get a taxi." He left.

Fowler was wondering how much alcohol he would need for him to forget, when somebody took Carslake's place. It was the woman who'd bumped into him earlier.

"You're looking sad, lover," she said.

"I am."

"Maybe I can help?"

"I'm sure we'll be able to come to some sort of arrangement."

The woman grinned at him. "I'm Candy."

"Yes, you are."

Nine

Now Jason Harwood was hunched over the table in interview room four, his nose inches away from the surface, displaying thinning hair on his crown. Gray took a seat opposite.

After starting the recording, stating his and Worthington's presence along with the appointed duty lawyer, Arthur Brand, Gray pushed a cup of coffee Harwood's way, spat out of a vending machine into a plastic cup a few minutes ago. Harwood had complained all the way over from Ramsgate and during the booking-in process that he hadn't had a chance to get a drink. Now he ignored it.

Gray placed a photograph of the stabbing victim next to the cup. "Do you recognise this man, Mr Harwood?"

Harwood lifted his eyes up. "Bloke who got murdered the other night. Saw it on the TV."

Gray left the image in place. "What about this?" He put the glove found at the crime scene onto the table. It was encased in a clear plastic evidence bag.

"It's a glove."

"Does it belong to you?"

Harwood shrugged. "Dunno."

Gray added another bagged glove to the first, a left and a right. A matched pair. "We found this one in your flat."

"So what?"

"And the other a few feet away from the murdered man. Your DNA was discovered inside. I'd bet when we analyse this," Gray tapped the glove from Harwood's flat, "we get the same result."

Harwood snapped his head up and looked at Gray properly for the first time, before turning to his lawyer. "What's he saying?"

Gray spoke before Brand could. "This item found at the scene of a murder belongs to you, Mr Harwood. Can you explain how your glove ended up in Union Row?"

"No way!" Harwood sat bolt upright. "This is bullshit! I didn't kill no one!" He turned to Brand again. "Tell him that this is bullshit!"

"Where were you between nine-thirty and eleven pm two nights ago?"

"Wednesday?"

"That's right."

Harwood considered the question for a few moments. His face lit up. "I was in the pub! Having a drink with some mates."

"Really."

"Yeah! Go there, check the cameras. That'll prove where I was."

"Which pub was this Mr Harwood?"

"The Windmill on Newington Road."

Gray knew it. "Okay, we'll do so. Interview terminated."

"I'm innocent, mate." Harwood was elated. "You've got the wrong man."

Gray left the room, got a uniform to return Harwood to his cell. When it was just him and Worthington, Gray said, "What do you think?"

"He seemed pretty convincing."

Gray felt the same. His gut told him something was wrong here. "Go down there, see whatever imagery you can get and bring it straight back."

"No problem," said Worthington. However, Gray thought it was very much a problem.

WORTHINGTON RETURNED well within an hour. He and Gray entered one of the meeting rooms to play the video recording straight onto a TV screen via a laptop.

"They've several cameras," said Worthington. "Inside and outside. The landlord said they'd had some trouble in the past and had them installed by the brewery."

Gray twirled a pen in his fingers while he waited. Soon a view from behind the bar came up. There were several people at the bar, waiting to be served. A man walked in through the door, waved at someone offscreen he must have known and leaned on the bar, awaiting his turn. The new entrant was Jason Harwood. The time stamp said 21.02.

"Bloody hell," said Gray, chewing on his pen. "How long was he there for?"

Worthington wound on. Harwood returned to the bar several more times. Damian Parker was present too. At 22.07, Worthington paused the playback as Harwood headed outside.

Gray sat forward. "Where's he going?" He remained hopeful. Margate was just a short taxi ride from Ramsgate. The timing would be tight, but feasible.

"Another feed picks him up," said Worthington.

Harwood was out the front of the pub. He sparked up a cigarette, chatting with a couple of fellow smokers.

"Now what?" asked Gray.

"That's it. He finishes the cigarette before going back inside for another pint and then leaving."

"What time?"

"22.29."

Gray threw the pen down on the table. "He's not our man."

"Doesn't seem so, sir. Not on this basis."

"So how the hell did a glove with his DNA on end up in our crime scene?"

Worthington shrugged.

"Let him go. In the meantime, I'd better give the DCI an update. Then we'll reconvene as a team and work out what we do from here."

"Okay, sir." Worthington left Gray alone.

Hamson would not be pleased. A seeming slam dunk earlier this morning had actually turned out to be an own goal.

"This is a bloody mess," said Gray. But there was nobody to hear it. He had an idea though. Maybe the public could help.

He headed upstairs to give Hamson the bad news. "It's not Harwood. He has an alibi."

"What about the glove?"

"A red herring."

"You said..."

"I know what I said, Von. I was wrong."

Hamson ran her fingers through her hair, holding her hands to her head. If Sylvia were still here she'd be listening at the door right now, enjoying Gray's plight.

"What did you want me to do? The evidence said bring him in, so we did. The evidence also said, release him. He has an alibi and we have absolutely no choice."

"I know."

"And I kept you up to date all the way through."

"I know that too and saying so doesn't help, Sol. I thought we had him."

"I'm as angry as you are."

"But it's not you who has to tell Marsh a suspect isn't one anymore."

"Playing politics again, Von? Dangerous game running to the boss every time something breaks."

Hamson eyed Gray. He'd gone too far. "And what are you doing right now?"

Gray held his hands up.

Hamson flopped back in her chair. "Where next?"

"I want to hold a press conference, see if anybody out there knows something."

"Go ahead if you think it'll help."

"Frankly, right now I'm all out of ideas."

"Just ensure Bethany is fully involved."

Gray rolled his eyes. Bethany Underwood was the station's Press Officer, a bleach-blonde waif who ran on nervous energy, constantly on the brink of flipping out.

"Sol," warned Hamson. She knew his feelings about Underwood all too well.

"Okay, it'll be the first thing I do when I leave here."

"Off you go then."

Gray tugged his forelock as he backed out of the office, bowing. His phone rang as he was descending the stairs. Pennance.

"Could my day be made any worse?" asked Gray.

"Charming."

"Sorry, it's been a disastrous morning so far. I thought we had a suspect for the murder, but it turns out he has an alibi."

"I've some useful information then. A heads up on the name of your dead man before it comes through officially. We tracked him down. It took a while."

"Go on."

"His name is LaShaun Oakley."

"Sounds like a brand of sunglasses."

"Very funny." But Pennance wasn't laughing. "Oakley didn't have a record, which explains why you couldn't find him on the database."

Yarrow had been right – a clean skin. "How did you find him?" asked Gray.

"I guess you're familiar with Pupil Referral Units?"

"Where kids who get excluded from schools end up. We have them here too, Marcus."

"Right, they're becoming fertile hunting grounds for the gangs. Spotting vulnerable kids then effectively grooming them with crap like fizzy drinks, fast food or trainers."

"Wonderful."

"Two of our team went through all the photos we had on file of referred children and eventually one matched. Oakley was from London; Enfield to be precise. A couple of colleagues went over to his parents' house earlier today. To say they were shocked at his death was an understatement."

"Poor bastards." Knife crime was blighting the youth of the country, London in particular. "Were they aware of his movements?"

"They couldn't understand why he'd be in Ramsgate. At first they didn't accept it was their son. His behaviour sounded totally alien. He'd been gone a few days but Oakley had said he was heading off with some friends across the city, not to Kent. That's all really."

"Thanks for letting me know, I appreciate it."

"You should get a report soon. Good luck."

Pennance rang off. A little more of the puzzle was filled in but there was still a distinct lack of clarity. Gray headed to his desk and repeated the process of scanning through social media apps to learn what he could about Oakley. Unlike Harwood, Oakley had a presence on all the major platforms. Gray's first impression was that Oakley appeared a normal guy, regularly out with friends, smiling in photographs. He didn't appear to be a dealer; somebody who sold Class As which ruined the lives of many, while enriching a few. But maybe that was the point.

Worthington was at his desk. Gray stood over him, and Worthington looked up. "We've a name for the Union Row victim," Gray told him. "LaShaun Oakley. I've had a quick look over his social media stuff. Get digging would you? I'm going to check out the crime scene again."

Ten

Now Gray decided to walk. It wasn't far to Union Row and he needed to think. He headed down Fort Crescent, past the Turner Contemporary gallery, before entering King Street, which marked the outer edge of the Old Town, an upcoming Hipster area of cafes and antique shops.

Gray remembered that he hadn't spoken to Underwood about setting up the press conference, too taken with talking to Pennance. That delight would have to await his return.

He cut across Market Place, past the English Flag, a pub which never seemed to close, and the last bastion against gentrification. Despite it being a dump and less than welcoming to the law-abiding, Gray was briefly tempted to go in for a beer.

The knockback over Harwood's apparent guilt had been hard to take. Given the DNA evidence from the glove, Gray had been convinced they had their man and he was thoroughly puzzled as to what had gone wrong. Another few hundred yards along Lombard Street, and Gray crossed through the boundary of the Old Town, emerging onto the busy road which ran past Morrisons.

At Union Row, Gray stopped. The police tape had been removed. The area was back to normal, people going about their business as if nothing had happened, no one had died. Two vans with the Iceland livery on their side were parked next to the rear entrance, being loaded for upcoming deliveries.

A uniformed PC stood at the alley's mouth. "Afternoon, sir," he said. It was Boughton, the local PC, wearing the thin, standard-issue short-sleeved shirt as usual. If shorts were allowed Gray reckoned Boughton would have those on too.

"Damian, how's things?"

"Pissed off, if you must know, sir. I hear the suspect has been released." The jungle drums beat quickly.

Gray sighed. "He had a concrete alibi."

"I don't like there being an unsolved murder on my patch."

"Me neither."

"Pardon me, sir." Boughton looked over Gray's shoulder. He held out a photo of Oakley, the one Gray had taken from Facebook. "Do you recognise this person?"

A passer-by glanced down at the image and shook his head without breaking stride.

"Nobody tells me jack shit about this guy," said Boughton.

"Oakley was here less than a day."

"And not one person had any interaction with him?" Boughton shook his head. "I find that very sad, sir."

Gray did too. "People don't look out for strangers anymore."

"That's our job, isn't it?"

"I guess so."

"What do you reckon it was then, sir? Wrong time, wrong place?"

"Given the CCTV footage, I think he was targeted. At least one person knew him. Or what he was, at least."

"Sweat and tears, sir, sweat and tears. That'll get us the answer. Are you here to take another look at the scene?"

"I just want to see if it sparks any ideas. Because at the moment I'm blank."

"I'll leave you to it, sir. Let me know if I can help."

Gray moved forward, pausing again near where Oakley had bled out. Like standing on a grave in a churchyard, Gray didn't really want to be on the exact spot, even though many pairs of feet would doubtless have crossed the patch. Oakley's blood had been washed away. The efforts of the paramedics forgotten. It was as if he'd never existed.

"Excuse me." Gray glanced up. A woman with a double buggy wanted to pass and he was blocking the way. He backed up against the wall. She walked on, giving him a strange look and no thanks. He lingered for a while longer, remembering the young man lying there.

Under Boughton's watchful eye, Gray headed back onto Union Row in reverse, following the route Oakley had taken in his final moments to where the murdered man had briefly lived, if that's what it could be called. As Gray glanced up and down the road, he realised he had nothing new. Beyond the scattergun approach of a press conference, Gray didn't know how he could find Oakley's killer.

With poetic justice, it began to rain. If there was a romantic side left to Gray, the supposition would be tears from on high at a wasted life. However, he was a pragmatist. Somebody had wanted Oakley dead. It sent a message, but from whom and to whom? He didn't know.

Yet.

He decided to head back to the station. When he passed the alley, Boughton was deep in conversation with a member of the public and didn't notice Gray. Focus – that was what Boughton possessed.

All Gray could do was keep pressing on. Sweat and tears, Boughton had said, mixed in with Oakley's blood.

Eleven

Now

While Gray waited for the gates to the underground car park beneath the complex of flats he lived in to open, he rubbed his forehead. The rest of his day had proven to be long and fruitless. A follow-up team meeting to discuss so-called progress hadn't gone well. Like Gray, the rest of the team was bereft of ideas, deflated and angry. The presence of the glove was particularly puzzling. Gray had wondered out loud if it was a plant to distract the investigation. The taping up of the knife handle pointed to particularly careful planning.

And Bethany Underwood, when Gray had found her, was her usual pleasurable self. She'd chewed her nails even more than usual when Gray asked her to organise for the newspapers and television to come in about Oakley's murder. Despite it being her job to do so, she appeared less than pleased. In the end, Gray had whipped off an email to her, copied to Hamson, to ensure the conference was scheduled for tomorrow because the following day the Pivot raids were planned. From past experience of major operations, Gray knew the station would be chaos, whether the raids were successful or not.

He jumped at the knock on his window.

It took him a moment to realise the person staring back at him. Hope. His daughter smiled at him, made a "wind your window down" motion, even though cars hadn't had handles for years. For a moment he forgot where the button was, he was so surprised.

"Hi, Dad," she said when the window was halfway.

"Hope, what are you...?" Gray's question was cut off by the bleep of a horn. He glanced in the rear-view mirror. Another car, wanting to access the garage. "Don't move," he said to Hope.

He drove inside, parked and walked as fast as he could back to the pavement. Hope was sitting on the low wall which encircled the flats. As Gray approached, she stood and flung herself into his arms.

"Oh, Dad." She began to sob into his shoulder. It was then he grasped that she had a large suitcase with her.

IT TOOK A FEW MINUTES to calm Hope down, during which Gray received several looks from passers-by, from intrigued to sympathetic. Eventually, he moved Hope upstairs; the two of them and her luggage barely fitting into the tiny lift.

Inside the flat, Hope said, "Can I get a drink, Dad? It's been a long day."

"Sure, make yourself at home."

"Where's your bathroom?"

Gray pointed her in the right direction, then got the kettle busy. While he was pouring hot water onto coffee grounds in a French press he heard the toilet flush. A few moments later Hope appeared in the kitchen doorway and leaned against the jamb.

"Milk and one sugar, isn't it?" asked Gray.

"Good memory."

"I don't forget much." He didn't add that this ability was as much a curse as a blessing.

"But can I have a cup of tea? Green if you have it."

"Sorry, I should have asked." He rummaged around for the box, found it, put a bag into a cup and poured water into it. He handed her the mug.

"Thanks," she said.

"Let's sit on the balcony," said Gray. Hope nodded.

Gray slid open one of the floor-to-ceiling doors. It moved easily on well-oiled runners. At Wyatt's insistence he'd recently bought a second chair and a couple of cushions to improve the comfort of the wooden-slatted furniture. Both chairs faced out to sea. Hope put her mug down on the small round table and leaned over the balcony railing. She glanced up and down the esplanade which ran along the clifftop immediately beneath them. Below that were the sands of Louisa Bay, a popular tourist spot with its own permanent beachfront café. The bacon sandwiches were good, the coffee, however, was instant.

"All these years living here, yet it's funny looking at a familiar outlook from a different perspective."

"I know." Gray had thought the same when he'd viewed the flat.

"Broadstairs has barely changed."

"It never does." A few shops came and went, restaurants closed and reopened under different names, but that was about all. The centre was tightly packed and much of it was under a conservation order from the council, so it was difficult to alter the buildings or layout. Gray owned a book containing old photos of the town dating back to Victorian times and it was much the same even then.

"I'll have to buy some flip flops," said Hope. "It's usually wellington boots or walking shoes in Edinburgh."

"Is this an impromptu holiday?" It was obvious something was up, but Gray wanted whatever the issue was to come out as and when Hope was ready.

She sagged into one of the chairs. "No. Well, I mean yes, sort of. I needed to get away from Hamish, from Scotland. I didn't want to impose on Grandma."

"You did the right thing and you're always welcome here. It's great to see you."

Hope smiled weakly. "Do you mind if I lie down? I'm a bit tired from the journey."

"No problem at all. I'll show you the spare room. The bed needs making up first."

"I'll give you a hand."

"I can cope."

Once Hope was settled, her case taking up quite a bit of space in the small bedroom, Gray retreated outside again. He put his feet up on the other chair, stretching out. He wondered what had brought Hope to him. Either relationship, job or money. The same motivations for criminal behaviour.

But part of him didn't mind what the reason was. She was here and she'd chosen him to escape to.

His phone rang. Wyatt. "Hi, how are you?" she asked.

"Pretty good, thanks."

"Glad to hear it." She sounded taken aback, like she'd expected him to be gloomy. "I've got a bottle of wine. I can bring it over or you can come to mine?"

"Sorry Emily, I can't. Not tonight."

"Oh, that's a pity." The disappointment was obvious in her tone. "Why?"

"I've got a guest."

"The surprises keep on coming, Sol. Can I ask who? Is it Yvonne?"

Gray laughed. "That's ridiculous."

"I shouldn't have asked. All we're doing is sleeping together."

"I don't mind."

"Which? Sleeping together or telling me who's in your bed?"

"Neither, both. Oh, I don't know!"

Wyatt laughed. "Men, you're all so easily confused."

"It's my daughter, Hope. She turned up unexpectedly."

"Oh God, sorry."

"What for?"

"Taking the mickey!"

"No problem."

"How is she? She lives in Edinburgh, right?"

"I've no idea, and she does. She gave no warning and hasn't told me anything. It's all a bit of a shock."

"Well that's great, although it's a shame I'll have to drink all this wine myself."

"I'll make it up to you."

"You'd better. See you tomorrow at the office. Faces back on."

"Absolutely." Wyatt disconnected.

"Who was that?" Hope was standing in the doorway, dressed in pyjamas and a robe. "Sorry," she said. "I didn't mean to startle you."

"It's okay." He placed his phone on the table. "I thought you were down for the night."

"You make me sound like a baby."

"Just a turn of phrase."

Gray moved his feet to allow Hope to sit. "I'm sorry for landing on you like this. I'd nowhere else to turn."

"It's no problem, what's the matter?"

She leaned forward, hands in lap. "I'm pregnant." Gray sat open-mouthed for a few moments. Hope filled the pause, said, "I didn't know how else to tell you."

"That's fantastic news!" Gray gave her a hug. She was stiff and immobile. He remembered her earlier upset. "Isn't it?"

She burst into tears again. Gray sat, unsure what to do, how to react. Then said, "I'll make you another cup of tea."

Gray filled the kettle and turned it on. He was going to be a grandfather. It was difficult for his already cluttered mind to fathom. He went back onto the balcony. Hope was twisted on her seat, looking out to sea, one arm on the railing, chin in hand. He put the cups down.

"What does Hamish think?"

"He really wants me to have it. He's got two children from a previous relationship but would love to have more."

"So, what's the problem?"

"I am," said Hope. "I'm not sure I could cope with being a mum. I'm still at University, for God's sake! I told Hamish what I thought. We argued about it and I left."

"When are you due?"

"The first of November."

"Your mum's birthday." Gray hugged her again. This time she softened and folded into him. "Whatever happens, whatever decision you make, everything will be all right. I'll make sure."

"Do you promise, Dad?"

"Cross my heart."

Twelve

Now Gray had to admit that, despite being a bag of nerves, when push came to shove Bethany Underwood was a mean co-ordinator. He was standing to the rear of the press room, watching the Press Officer marshall the correspondents into some form of order. Presently, she was giving a grizzled TV cameraman the third degree about where to position his equipment. There was no favouritism in Underwood's world.

Once she'd finished verbally battering the cameraman, she strode over to Gray. Her blonde hair was as frizzy as ever and she'd taken to adopting the fashion trend of plucking her eyebrows and drawing them back in again, seemingly with a thick, black crayon.

"Bloody well think they can do as they like," she said.

The room was structured with a degree of symmetry: a table at the very front with seats and a microphone, which Gray would shortly be behind; then four rows of chairs for the journalists, where many already sat, flicking through the press pack handed to them when they entered; and finally, television cameras and recording equipment strung out at the rear.

"I'm impressed, Bethany," said Gray.

Underwood gave him a funny, disbelieving glance. "Thanks." She sounded suspicious. "You're on in five minutes. Remember, deliver your patter then open up for questions. You can run as long as you want but this lot get bored quickly. Many of them will be after the salacious. My offer to cut them off at the knees should they piss about remains, Solomon." Underwood refused to shorten Gray's name and he'd long given up telling her it was all right to do so.

"You know what, Bethany, I accept." Given what Gray had just witnessed it might be a wise idea to have the cavalry standing by.

"I'll be over there." Underwood pointed a nicotine-stained finger – the result of smoking roll ups – to where Hamson was standing. Hamson had refused Gray's suggestion that she, as the senior officer, hold the press conference. Gray was in charge of the case. "Against the wall and just out of camera shot but well and truly in their eyeline," said Underwood. "When you get to the questions, I'll shake my head if any of the reporters should be avoided." She checked her watch again. "Right, go and take your place. Accept no shit, Solomon."

Gray headed to the front, pulled out a chair and sat. He squinted under the harsh glare of a light directed into his eyes. Moments later the beam was shifted slightly, following Underwood's snippy direction. Hamson gave him a thumbs-up. Underwood gave the okay sign, finger and thumb in a circle.

"Ladies and gentlemen, I appreciate your time today. I've asked you here in order to make a public appeal for information regarding the murder of LaShaun Oakley." Gray held up Oakley's photo, one Worthington had pulled off social media. It was reproduced in the press pack too. Cameras snapped away. "He was stabbed to death three days ago at 10.39pm in Union Row, Margate." Gray lowered the picture. "Mr Oakley had only just arrived in our town from London. As yet, we have not identified his attacker and I am appealing for information. Somebody out there knows something that can help us. I ask that if you have anything to say, no matter how trivial, please do so and I assure you it will be treated in the strictest confidence. I'll take questions now."

A young woman in the centre raised her hand. Gray glanced towards Underwood. She nodded.

"Felicity Rainoake of the *Express*. Is it true that a person was arrested yesterday in connection with Mr Oakley's murder?"

"A man was helping us with our enquiries, but we've since released him."

"Mr Harwood, correct?"

"That's right."

"You were Mr Harwood's arresting officer?"

"I was but the purpose of this conference is to appeal for witnesses to the murder."

"Mr Harwood is claiming wrongful arrest."

"We had good cause to bring Mr Harwood in and I believe we followed due procedure."

Other hands went up, as well as Rainoake's. Gray bypassed the *Express* reporter and pointed to a grey-haired man wearing an ill-fitting suit.

"Adam Payton, *The Guardian*. Do you have any further leads?"

"We are pursuing multiple lines of investigation. This is a fast-moving and complex case."

"Which means you don't have anything," said Payton.

"Nothing I can discuss at this time."

"Mr Harwood is also claiming he was mistreated during his arrest." It was Rainoake again, not waiting to be asked. Underwood was making a throat-cutting motion with her hand.

"That's not something I'm aware of," said Gray.

"We have an exclusive interview with Mr Harwood which will be published tomorrow."

"I look forward to reading it. Are there any more questions?"

But now Underwood stepped in. "Thank you for your time everyone," she said to the reporters, ending the press conference. It was about the fastest press conference he'd ever attended. A few more photographs were snapped while the crowd of reporters began to break up. Hamson headed forward and paused beside Underwood. Gray joined them.

"You got ambushed there," said Underwood.

"It didn't quite go as I intended." Gray turned to Hamson. "Has Harwood made his complaint official?"

"Not to my knowledge," said Hamson.

"Bloody press," said Underwood. Gray couldn't disagree. "I've always said they're bastards."

"Anyway," said Hamson, "I'll find out if anything is going on with Harwood. And let's see what this article says. Until then we've got Pivot to deal with."

Thirteen

Now "Thank you for coming, everyone," said Yarrow.

The Incident Room was full, every chair taken. All of CID and most of uniform were present. Yarrow stood at the front, holding court, Hamson to one side, leaning against the wall. As Gray preferred, he was at the back, out of the way, Fowler adjacent to him.

"After months of hard work, the day of reckoning is nearly upon us," said Yarrow.

"Bit biblical," mumbled Fowler. Gray had to agree. It made a change for Gray to be with Fowler again. He'd hardly seen his friend these last few months. Pivot had taken a significant toll on his free time.

Yarrow continued. "We have the warrants signed off by a judge, so tomorrow morning, bright and early, we're going into a number of properties to take down the dealers who have blighted your town for months. These guys." Yarrow turned and pointed to a double row of A3 laminated cards, each with a photo, name and series of particulars against them, affixed to the wall. "But more about them shortly. I can see there are a few faces who haven't attended previous briefings, but I guess someone had to keep the station running while we interfered." Yarrow gave a self-deprecating chuckle. Most of his team joined in. Hamson retained a straight face.

"So, apologies to those who've heard this before, but it's important everyone has the same facts. You're already aware what a County Line is and its intent. God knows, you've experienced enough of the fallout recently. However, a key feature is the use of a mobile phone which is central to the customer base. Typically, this phone is located in the urban hub, London in this case. Periodically, a group message is sent out to the entire customer base to advertise the availability of drugs, and orders are placed back to this line in response from these said customers. It's like a massive WhatsApp group chat, but about Class A's." Yarrow got another laugh. "A relay system sends the orders on to another number followed by the individual dealers in the marketplace. Then the dealers go out and ply their trade. A line can typically make three to five grand per day. That's big money in anyone's book. Except maybe a Premiership football player." More chuckles.

"The phone number itself acquires a value, as a business does. Actually, that's what this is to these people, a commercial venture, but one where the employer has no regard for its staff and the staff have no rights. There are cases of individual numbers being sold for tens of thousands of pounds. It's like a franchise. The developed process is sold on to others for them to implement elsewhere in the country. The phones are the key. So, when we hit the properties, I want you to look out for every bit of tech you can spot, particularly mobiles. They tend to use old clunkers from a decade ago. No smartphones here. All clear?"

Nods from around the room.

"As I said, the bastards who run the lines don't care for anyone. At several locations we fully expect to find users. Like this one." Yarrow pulled one of the bios off the wall and held it up above his head for all to see. "Eloise Nunes. She takes a lot, sells a little, including herself." Yarrow stuck the bio back on the wall in its place.

"Often there's more than one address from which the narcotics are spread out across the area, reducing the impact on the whole supply chain should a successful police raid occur. Drug movements are far more frequent and the value significantly less – i.e. if you get caught with them, the sentence is much reduced. So don't anticipate finding half a ton of crack. It'll be a few wraps. But the objective here isn't volume, it's value; to take out multiples of these small chunks of Class A's.

"Thanks to your sterling work, we believe we've identified pretty much every dealer, every property, cuckooed or not, and every seemingly legitimate business front across Ramsgate, Broadstairs and Margate. So bloody well done. Mike Fowler was particularly upset when he found out his favourite burger joint was also distributing gear." More laughs, Fowler joined in.

A serious expression crossed Yarrow's face. "Now, a word of caution. County Lines gangs employ a high level of violence and intimidation to gain and build markets. There are at least eight lines running into Margate. That's eight streams being used to pump junk into people's veins. Think about it. 'Taxing' is the marking or injuring of a gang member who's done wrong to discourage others from doing the same. For example, one man had his hand severed and both legs broken for snorting the drugs he was supposed to be selling and spending the proceeds from whatever didn't go up his nose.

"Kids are used to run drugs and money. They're usually anywhere between thirteen and eighteen, the majority being fifteen to seventeen. Young children are used to entice others in via social media with the opportunity of earning large sums of money – a promise which turns out to be a lie. Often family members are threatened or intimidated. And there's 'debt bondage' where individuals work for free to pay back what they owe. Not that runners earn much. A few hundred quid a week and they take most of the risk of being caught. Women may be forced into sex. And woe betide anyone who grasses. That's the type of people we're dealing with here.

"There's a regular transition of individuals between the urban and rural centre to bring in more drugs and transport cash. Typically, movements are by train, although, as funds increase, a shift to vehicular access increases. The people they're using don't stay long; a few weeks to a month, to prevent the individuals becoming known to us. So, we may find injured or scared people in the properties who should to be treated with care.

"The dealers need to keep the people they're exploiting in line. The use of knives, firearms, baseball bats and more recently acid and other corrosives, is increasingly common. We're seeing assault, kidnapping and burglary. Sometimes murder. There was an example earlier this week with LaShaun Oakley, who was stabbed to death. DCI Hamson has asked that everyone we arrest be questioned about Oakley.

"Once we've gone in and taken down the dealers there's still going to be a huge amount of work for all of us do. There will be an awful lot of junkies wandering the streets looking for someone to buy their fix from. Unfortunately, another dealer is always waiting in the wings to fill the gap. Therefore, after tomorrow this isn't over by a long chalk. But together we'll have put a big, nasty hole in Thanet's drugs supply.

"Right, I've done enough lecturing. You've all been split into teams. The details of who's in what group are on the wall over there." Yarrow pointed to several pieces of A4 paper beside Hamson. "See who you're with, who's your leader and the address you'll be at. Then, familiarise yourselves with our targets." Yarrow hiked a thumb at the laminated photos.

"These buggers move around the properties, so you could be taking down any one of them. Be here 4am sharp tomorrow. We're going in hard and fast at 5am. The assaults will be co-ordinated. Once we take one place, the jungle drums will start up and before we know it our targets will have flown. At the same time, our colleagues in London will be hitting a number of associated properties.

"My objective is to have each and every one of these scrotes in the cells by this time tomorrow. Nobody gets away. Okay?" Yarrow looked around the room, got the nods he wanted. "Thank you everybody and good luck. See you in the morning."

The room broke into a buzz of conversation and disorder as en-masse the team shifted towards the team list and the crib sheets. Gray already knew which team he was in; he'd helped build the list.

Damian Parker was Gray's primary target. He'd cuckooed the female user Yarrow had mentioned, Eloise Nunes. Parker was one of the more senior people in the set-up. He was a local, though regularly travelled between the capital and Thanet transporting cash and drugs. They anticipated he'd have information which would lead to further arrests. Gray crossed over to Parker's photo, took in the man's scowl, his attempt to look tough. Otherwise Parker appeared entirely normal. A reasonably well-to-do guy in his mid-twenties with a neat haircut and wearing decent clothes. Not the usual type expected to be a drug runner. But they'd captured footage of Parker doing a deal in broad daylight.

"It's going to be beautiful," said Fowler, who'd sidled up beside Gray. When in uniform, Fowler had always been up for a confrontation. He'd become expert at wielding the battering ram. "All that smashing wood and breaking glass. They're not going to have a clue what's hit them."

Fourteen

Now Gray was wired. It was 4.50am and he'd been up over an hour already. He and eight other officers sat tight in the back of an unmarked van, parked around the corner from the target address. The closeness of the bodies made it warm inside; Gray had people either side of him, knees touching. The guy opposite was jiggling his leg. Gray understood why. Only ten minutes till they were due to go in.

Gray wore the basic uniform: black trousers, shirt and a stab vest. In his lap was a black baseball cap with POLICE written across the front. Half the team were equipped in gear the average bystander would associate with a riot; body armour and helmets. The battering ram, a bright red cylinder with a carrying handle, lay on the floor at their feet.

The radio crackled. Yarrow said, "Move into position." The driver up front started the van's engine and inched forward. Gray felt the vehicle turn, coasting out of gear or the driver had his foot on the clutch.

Just five minutes before the deadline.

The van came to a slow halt. Gray moved to the rear with difficulty. The stab vest was heavy and rigid. The utility belt round his waist weighed about the same as the vest. In all it was bloody uncomfortable. Gray popped the door open and stepped down, landing silently. He glanced both ways along the street. Nobody was around, not even an early morning dog walker.

Parker occupied a terraced house on Hengist Avenue, named after a Viking raider who'd landed in Broadstairs a thousand years ago, a fact well known locally. The road was on the Millmead Estate. The van had drawn up beneath a streetlight, bulb blown, across a driveway on which a car was parked.

The road was narrow, vehicles bumper-to-bumper on both sides, space a premium. Several cars had broken wing mirrors. Gray crooked his finger. The others stepped down. One guy in riot gear patted the ram like it was a pet before he lifted it out. Gray pointed to the house they wanted which was a little further down the hill.

Two minutes, but they'd only go when Yarrow gave the word.

The house was a narrow three-storey end-terrace set back a few feet from the pavement, pointlessly delineated by a low wall only a couple of feet high. A metal gate was off its hinges and propped against the downstairs bay window, slowly rusting. The officer with the tubular metal ram, accompanied by a colleague, lurked by the front door, hedged in by two large plastic wheelie bins. A further two uniforms hung back on the pavement, ready to crowd in once the door was gone. Gray pointed for two more to head along the alley in case Parker ducked out the back. Gray took up position on the corner, able to keep an eye on proceedings on both the alley and the front.

The shout came in from Yarrow over the radio. "Go, go, go!"

"Do it," ordered Gray.

The officer swung back the battering ram and belted the mass into the door. Sometimes doors fell first time. Not now. It barely budged. The cop crashed the ram again, not needing to be told to do so. A third, then a fourth time. On the fifth, Gray heard a splintering. And the sound of a window opening.

A leg protruded from a first-floor window. Finally, the door collapsed under the onslaught with a huge crack. The shout, "Police!" went up as a second leg came out and then the rest of the person. Parker, wearing shorts, trainers and a hoody, dangled from the windowsill for a moment before dropping to the ground.

Gray's colleagues were piling into the property while Parker was escaping.

"Stop where you are!" shouted Gray.

Parker swung around, caught sight of Gray and immediately turned in the opposite direction, down the alley. Gray started after him. He got ten feet by the time one of the uniforms Gray had sent to watch the rear emerged from the garden.

Parker paused, glanced over his shoulder. The PC, a stocky, short woman named Jones, was nearest. Parker reached inside the pocket of his hoody, pulled something out and flicked his wrist. There was the unmistakable snap of a baton extending.

Jones went for her own, but Parker stepped forward and swung fast. Jones raised her arm instinctively as Parker swung. The breaking of bone was audible. Jones screamed and went down.

Gray threw himself at Parker as he stood over Jones, barrelling the man over. Parker caught a foot on the prostrate Jones and hit the ground hard, the baton skittling away. The air went out of Parker's lungs with a whoosh.

But Parker was up quickly and kneeling on Gray, raining down blows with his fists. Gray held up his arms, trying to shield his face from Parker's knuckles. He took a couple on the forearms. Then Parker stood and attempted to put a boot into Gray's kidney. The stab vest absorbed the blow and Parker cried out in pain.

Gray rolled and got a grip on the man's ankle. Parker tried to tug himself away and break Gray's hold. Then Parker began to jerk, his arms and legs rigid, his mouth contorted. Gray let go immediately. A moment later Parker collapsed onto the ground, continuing to spasm.

"You okay, sir?" It was Jones, face as pale as milk, cradling her arm and holding a Taser.

"I'm fine," said Gray. He ached where Parker had punched him, but thankfully the vest had taken the worst of it. And compared to Jones' injury his were entirely minor. He slowly got to his feet.

Gray took the Taser from Jones. She said, "Can you cuff him, sir?"

"With pleasure." Gray unclipped a pair of handcuffs from Jones' belt. He bent down, rolled the still incapacitated Parker over, folded his hands behind his back and ratcheted the restraints.

"Let's get you some first aid," said Gray.

Jones shook her head. "I'm all right, sir."

"Bullshit, I heard the bone break from five feet away. Come on."

Gray pulled an unresisting Parker to his feet then led Jones to the front of the house, pushing Parker before him.

"Call an ambulance," said Gray to a uniform. "And book him for resisting arrest and assaulting a police officer." Gray shoved Parker forward. The PC took over, leading Parker to a nearby wagon.

The noise had woken the street up. Neighbours were out of their houses or at windows, curtains raised. A woman from next door, dressing gown tightly pulled around her ample frame, watched Parker being led to the van. As he passed she spat at him. "Good riddance, you bastard!" Parker recoiled, then went for the woman. The PC holding Parker struggled to restrain him. Gray and one other piled in and wrestled Parker into the van, slamming the door.

"I'll get you for that, you bitch!" shouted Parker through the grill. Gray closed it, containing Parker's rage. He hammered on the panels, but it was a futile protest.

"I've been telling you people for ages about Parker," said the neighbour in a lilting Caribbean accent before Gray could speak. "About time you came and got him, selling that shit to children around here. It's disgusting."

"Would you prepared to be a witness if Mr Parker goes to court?" asked Gray.

"Mister? Don't be giving him no title, he's scum! Of course I'll be a witness. We don't want him round here no more."

"Thank you. What's your name, please?"

"It's Alvita Venables."

"I'll have someone come and speak to you."

Gray returned his attention to the property as the woman headed back inside. The front door had been pulled away from its hinges and joined the gate in the front garden. The jamb was a mess. There had been at least three locks and a couple of bolts.

The door itself was backed with sheet metal. It had been the surrounding frame which had eventually failed, rather than the door itself.

Gray stepped into a small hallway with peeling wallpaper. A naked bulb burned above. A front room was immediately to the right; stairs beyond and a corridor. Another closed door to what could have been the dining room, behind which a dog was barking, its tone low, deep and continuous. Further along a kitchen which smelt of chip fat.

"Big bastard," said Herron, a recently promoted sergeant. He'd been the one swinging the ram. He was a big bastard himself, shaven-headed, tattooed. "Staffordshire Bull Terrier." Dog rescue centres were full of the breed these days as they fell out of favour due to their aggressive reputation. Photos of staffies in the newspaper with members of far-right groups like the English Defence League hadn't helped.

"Have you called the K9 unit?"

"Bit early for them, Guv," said Herron with a grin. Gray laughed, some of the tension coming off.

"Have we found anything yet?"

"Sir, you need to see this!" A shout from the upper floor, CID leaning over the bannister.

Gray climbed the stairs, the carpet worn and dirty. There was an odour about the place too. Not just the dog, but damp and decay. On the next floor were two bedrooms and a bathroom, all the doors wide open. In one room a cop was squatting down beside a bed. Gray entered briefly. There was a form huddled under the covers. Eloise Nunes. Drug paraphernalia was scattered across the floor. Gray placed his feet carefully as he walked.

"She doesn't want to move, sir," said the cop speaking with Nunes.

"Get her healthcare worker, see if they can help."

Across the hallway two cops wearing gloves were searching. The window was wide open. This was where Parker had escaped from. A couple of phones, already bagged, lay on the mattress. More than likely the mobiles Yarrow had made such a point about yesterday. Gray picked one up, pressed a couple of keys through the plastic. A short stream of texts popped up, enquiries for drugs from customers. The numbers would prove vital to dealing with the wider network. Probably many of Parker's customers would be getting a visit from uniform soon.

Gray continued up the stairs. At the top of the house was an attic room, empty except for a table and a chair, several cops within.

"Thought you'd got lost, sir," said DC Robinson. He wore a T-shirt which displayed the Levi jeans logo stretched across his chest.

"Very funny," said Gray.

"This'll cheer you up," said Robinson. He indicated a cupboard set into the eaves. Gray looked closer. Beneath the floorboards was a stash of white powder in plastic bags. "Nunes told us it was here. She wanted to get some."

"Any money?" asked Gray.

"Virtually nothing, but a full load of gear."

Which meant Parker's most recent run to London had been to take back cash and bring in more merchandise to sell.

"Great. Keep looking; see what else turns up," said Gray. He headed back down the stairs and outside to call Yarrow. An ambulance had just arrived for Jones.

"How did it go, Sol?" asked Yarrow once the call connected.

"A bit messy, sir. But we got Parker, Nunes and a stash of drugs."

"Well done. Seems like we've pulled in just about everybody. Only the one empty property. Appears they scarpered a few hours before we arrived."

"One hundred per cent would have been a tough ask, sir."

"You're right, but it's irritating nevertheless. Anyway, well done, see you back at the station."

Gray slid his mobile into a pocket and headed over to the ambulance to ensure Jones was okay.

Fifteen

Now

Gray rubbed his eyes as he waited for the kettle. It was only just after 11.00am but already mind and body felt like it had been a full day. The lack of sleep and change in routine was fast catching up with him.

As the water began to roil Gray flicked the switch off, not wanting the temperature to reach boiling point. It burnt the coffee and ruined the taste. He felt a light touch on his arm. It was Wyatt.

"Don't worry," Wyatt smiled up at him, kept her voice low as she leaned in. "Nobody saw."

Gray couldn't help but look over his shoulder into the Detectives' Office. Not one person was paying them a blind bit of attention. "Sorry."

"Am I that embarrassing?"

"I'm just used to being talked about," said Gray. "I don't like to give anyone ammunition, particularly Mike."

"People might surprise you, Sol."

"Maybe." Gray doubted it. He poured water onto the grounds in a single-cup French press.

"How's Pivot going?"

"Really well." Gray was relieved to be back on a professional footing. He turned around. "I'm just about to interview Parker."

"You look tired."

"Knackered."

"Would it be okay if I popped over later? It would be nice to meet Hope."

"I'm not sure that's wise."

"Sorry to interrupt sir, we're waiting for you." It was Worthington, in the office entrance, beckoning him. "We're in Two." He left.

"Look, I'll tell you about it later." Wyatt's expression twisted into a frown. "Got to go. Help yourself to the coffee." Gray hurried away.

When he reached the interview room, Worthington pushed the door open, allowing Gray to enter first. Eloise Nunes sat hunched in her chair. She appeared worn and shabby. Her dyed pink hair was in disarray and pushed under a woollen hat; in places her locks stuck out at wild angles. She wore a stained dress, with a cardigan pulled over the top, one button done up but not in the right hole so the outfit was skewed. Her legs were bare, socks mismatched, and trainers, once white, were now grey.

Nunes' lawyer, a bespectacled man Gray didn't recognise, stood and shook both his and Worthington's hands. "Lesley Surtees," he said by way of introduction before retaking his seat.

Gray started the recorder, noted the time, date and everyone present. Nunes rocked in her chair. She scratched at a red mark at the corner of her mouth, then her arm. Coming down off a high; he'd need to watch that.

"How are you, Miss Nunes?" asked Gray.

"I'm a mess," she said, blowing out a stream of beery breath like she was releasing a demon. Gray heard the accent, her

Spanish heritage still present, her skin was pale, as if she never went outside. Gray had read her file. From a good background, travelled across the Channel a decade ago to teach her native tongue in a Broadstairs-based language school and somehow spiralled into trouble. Nunes lolled back in her chair and began to cry. After a few moments she cuffed the tears away. "Did you arrest Damian?"

"Yes."

"Good, he's a piece of *shit*."

Gray had an opinion, however not one he could express here and now. Instead he asked, "Does the residence where we found you and Mr Parker belong to you?"

"It's a council house, but the place is in my name."

"What was Mr Parker doing there?"

"We were sleeping together every now and then. A shag for a fix. At first it suited both of us. He promised me drugs if he could store some stuff there, just temporarily he said. Then one day he wouldn't leave. Moved his clothes into a spare room. Then his mates. Always in and out. I was powerless."

"We have evidence you've been dealing, Miss Nunes."

Surtees cut in. "Perhaps you should share this evidence with my client before making accusations, inspector."

However, Nunes shrugged. "I had to. I'm an addict, officer. I *need* to put that crap in my veins and he gave it to me. He forced me to screw him too, even though by then I didn't want to. Sometimes his mates, after I'd had a hit. He put me out on the streets to make some cash, which I just blew on gear. I'm not proud of what I've done, but I couldn't help myself." Nunes tried to grab Gray's hand, but he managed to withdraw it before she could take a grip. "I just want to be free. Can you help me? Get me clean?"

"There's a programme we can put you on, if you want."

"More than anything." Nunes covered her face with her hands and swayed back and forth.

"You'll likely pick up a sentence for dealing, Miss Nunes."

"You can't say that for sure, inspector," said Surtees. "Miss Nunes, you don't have to answer these questions."

"I want to," said Nunes. "I deserve this."

"Your call, Miss Nunes."

"I don't care," said Nunes. "As long as I'm away from them, I'll take it."

"One more thing," said Gray. "Do you know about the murder of a nineteen-year-old male four days ago by the name of LaShaun Oakley? He was a runner."

Nunes frowned, as if sifting through hazy memories. "I haven't been out the house for days."

"Has Mr Parker ever made any mention of Mr Oakley?"

"I don't think so."

"Okay. Thank you for your time, Miss Nunes." Gray was about to stop the recording but Nunes cut in.

"Though he did talk about a kid and his Line pissing on his business and how it was going to be stopped."

Gray withdrew his finger. "Go on."

Nunes shrugged. "I was lying on his bed after he'd, you know, finished with me, when his phone rang. He thought I was out of it. I usually am; it's the way I cope. He was on his phone to somebody, swearing his head off about doing the next one that got off the train. That's it really."

"You've been very helpful, Miss Nunes."

"You got any stuff?" Nunes leaned forward.

"We'll help you get clean, remember?"

Nunes nodded, head loose on her shoulders. Gray terminated the interview this time, called for a PC to take her back to the cells and show the lawyer out.

"Interesting," said Worthington when they were alone.

"Promising, yes. However, you know junkies will say anything to get what they want." Gray stood. "Let's go talk to Parker."

Sixteen

Now Worthington, with laptop and a folder under his arm, entered the adjacent interview room, Gray in his wake.

Parker was inclined back, his chair on two legs, pressed into a corner of the room, hands down the front of his trousers. He didn't bother to glance at Worthington and Gray, staring at the ceiling instead. The expression on his face spoke volumes. Bored tough guy without a concern in the world.

Parker's lawyer sat beside him; Alfie Lakehurst, one of the duty briefs, who appeared as ragged as Gray felt. Mussed hair, bags under the eyes, skewed tie, like he'd pulled an all-nighter. Apparently middle-aged, from the white patches in his brown beard.

Gray sat. Once he'd started the digital recorder running he said, "Assaulting a police officer is a serious charge, Mr Parker. As is resisting arrest."

Parker withdrew his attention from the interior decor, flicked his gaze from Worthington to Gray. "Wrongful arrest, bro." He shrugged. "And youse smashed down my door. Illegal entry. I'll sue you for both. Make myself a fortune." Parker brought his chair onto all four legs and nudged Lakehurst hard, smiled and nodded at him. "Am I right or am I right?" Lakehurst didn't reply, maintaining an admirably straight face.

Worthington opened up the folder he'd brought in, extracted a piece of paper and slid it across the desk. "For the benefit of the recording, I'm showing Mr Parker the warrant granting us entry to the property on Hengist Avenue. It's all above board."

Lakehurst scanned the document. "I agree."

Worthington took the paper back.

"The officer you struck is okay, by the way," said Gray, "I'm sure you'll be concerned about her welfare. She sustained a broken arm." Parker resumed his nonchalant stance, leaning the chair back, reviewing the ceiling. He didn't even bother to shrug. "The baton you had was police issue. Where did you get it, Mr Parker?"

"Found it. Lying around on the pavement. One of your lot must have dropped it. Careless bastards." Parker grinned.

"What's not so funny, is we discovered a quantity of crack cocaine and heroin in your house."

Worthington fanned several photos out on the table, showing the drugs beneath the floorboards, then out onto the carpet, arranged to demonstrate how much was present.

"Not my gaff, not my stuff. Belongs to the woman, right?" Parker snapped his fingers, as if trying and failing to recall her name.

"Eloise Nunes."

"Yeah."

"How do you know her?"

"We shag every now and again." Parker looked at Gray, gave a broad grin. "She can't get enough of me. Know what I mean? But she does my head in, dude. Being a junkie an' all."

"That's touching, Mr Parker."

"What can I say? I'm a lover man."

"So you deny the drugs belong to you?"

"That's what I said. Tell him, Alfie." Parker turned to Lakehurst. "Tell him I didn't do nothing."

Lakehurst gave Parker an irritated look. Clearly the lawyer wasn't enamoured with his client, though had to do his job. "Have you any evidence to back up your accusation, Inspector Gray?"

"Unfortunately for Mr Parker, yes."

Worthington lifted the lid of his laptop. The screen kicked into life and a window popped up. Worthington nudged at the integrated mouse pad, clicked the play arrow and a scene began. Parker, his attention grabbed, got close to the screen, eyes narrowed. It was footage of Parker doing a deal, handing over wraps in exchange for cash. It was over quickly, but Parker's features were clear even beneath the tightly drawn hood.

Concern leaked across Parker's face.

"We've had undercover surveillance on you for months, Mr Parker. This isn't the only recording in our possession. We have you coming and going from Miss Nunes' property and several others in the area, working with known dealers, all of whom are in cells next door to you, because we raided all of those as well. We've been collecting fingerprint evidence, so I fully expect to tie you into a fairly major drug dealing network. What do you have to say to that, Mr Parker?"

"Perhaps this would be a good time for me and my client to have a few moments together," said Lakehurst. Parker nodded vigorously in agreement.

"Be my guest." Gray stopped the playback. He and Worthington left the room.

"Parker knows he's screwed," said Worthington once they were standing in the corridor. Fowler passed by, escorting another prisoner arrested in the early hours to the adjacent room. He winked at Gray, clearly enjoying himself. Multiple interviews were underway, using up pretty much the station's entire resource.

"Agreed," said Gray. "I'll be back in a minute, I'm going to get another coffee. I need the kick." He stifled a yawn. "Parker can wait if he decides to talk again before I'm back. Want one?"

"I'm good, thanks."

When Gray reached the office, Wyatt wasn't there. He wanted to explain himself regarding his reluctance for her to come over. His half-finished cafetière was where he'd left it, lukewarm now. Nobody cleared anything up round here. Gray poured the drink into his mug, zapped it in the microwave for half a minute before he went back to Worthington.

"Sorted?" said Worthington. Gray held his mug up.

The door opened. "We're ready for you," said Lakehurst.

Parker appeared deflated. He sat with his head leaning on his arms on the table. Worthington raised an eyebrow at Gray. Often people started dealing for the money, without realising or accepting the risks. Gray would take a bet that Parker was one of the naive employees drawn in by the promise of easy money with no regard for the potential consequences. Consequences he was about to suffer.

Recorder restarted, Lakehurst said, "My client would like to make a statement."

"Okay," said Gray. "Go ahead."

Parker didn't immediately speak, as if gathering himself. "Look," he said eventually, all the fight gone from his tone. "I've a baby on the way and a toddler already, that's why I deal, to pay for the kids and their mums, all right?" The gangster language was dropped too.

"Which makes selling Class A drugs acceptable?"

"Well, it's fair enough, though?"

"Not really, no, Mr Parker."

"How long am I looking at?"

"Could be ten years."

"What?" Parker was clearly taken aback. His jaw hung open briefly, showing stained teeth. "For some dealing?"

"Constable Worthington and I had a very interesting conversation with Miss Nunes earlier. She said you were talking about murdering, and I quote, 'the next little bastard that gets off the train from London to piss on my patch.'"

Parker laughed. "She's a junkie. She'll say make any old crap up to get some gear."

"Miss Nunes was pretty convincing."

Parker sat back, crossed his arms and shook his head, appearing insulted. "Is that all you have? You make me laugh, you lot. It wasn't me."

"Meaning you know who did kill Mr Oakley?"

Parker unfolded his arms. "So what if I do? What's in it for me? You letting me walk out of here?"

"That's very unlikely."

"There you go, then. I'm done here. I'll admit to dealing, but you ain't pinning no murder on me." Parker turned to Lakehurst. "I want to go back to my cell."

Gray couldn't get another word from Parker so he granted his demand.

Seventeen

Now Gray headed to the canteen. He got a call while he was queueing.

Hamson. "Where are you, Sol?"

"The ubiquitously named restaurant."

"I'll be down in a few minutes. Grab me a tea, would you?"

Gray took two mugs to a table and awaited the DI's appearance. Of course, she took longer than she said, and Gray had almost finished his drink when she finally arrived.

"Sorry," she said. "It bloody never stops. Any useful leads on Oakley?"

"Possibly. One of the people we pulled in this morning, guy called Parker, may know something, but he's stitched up tight. Unless he gets a deal, of course. The woman he cuckooed, Eloise Nunes, made some noises about Parker's involvement, but she'd be an unreliable witness in my opinion."

"She's the junkie, right?"

"Yes."

"Then I agree with you. CPS probably wouldn't touch it. What's Parker looking for?"

"Freedom."

"Aren't we all?" Hamson laughed, a short, rueful snort. "Not a hope in hell."

"Pretty much what I said, though not as bluntly."

Hamson sank half her tea. "Let me think about it. If there's a chance of clearing up a murder, maybe we should come to a compromise."

"It's Nunes I feel sorry for. She's gone through a lot."

"I wouldn't waste any of your heart on her, Sol. Remember, somebody she sold gear to a few weeks ago suffered an overdose."

Before Gray could reply, he felt a slap on his shoulder, hard enough to have made him spill his drink had his cup not been almost empty. Fowler sat down beside him.

"Sorry about that, Sol," he said, and nodded at Hamson. "Guv."

"I'd better be going," said Hamson.

"No need to leave on my behalf."

"Don't flatter yourself," said Hamson as she pushed back her chair. "There's plenty to be getting on with."

"Screw you too," mumbled Fowler as Hamson strode away.

"I thought you pair were done with that?" asked Gray.

"Not you as well. What's up? You've a face like a dirty weekend."

"The Oakley murder, we've hit a solid dead end. Nunes, a woman sharing a house with Parker, made some noises that Parker may be involved. Of course, he's denying everything and she's not somebody I'd depend upon. Hamson's thinking of striking a bargain with him, though."

"Christ, she's even more of a fool than I took her to be if she thinks this Parker arsehole is actually going to give you anything. He's pulling your chain, Sol. You know it, I know it."

"Maybe, but we're stalled. Perhaps Parker really can help."

"Take my advice. Ignore him. If not, at least make him sweat until tomorrow."

"Maybe."

Eighteen

Now

If Gray had been tired this morning he was absolutely shattered now. He'd attempted to track down Wyatt several times during the day but on every occasion, something had dragged his attention away. Like the arrival of Superintendent Marsh, here to bask in the glory of a successful operation. But where had Marsh been when the real work was being done? Most likely in a meeting. In fact, he was in one now with Hamson. Gray wasn't invited.

Yarrow had announced that everyone was to assemble in the Incident Room at 7.00pm for a briefing. It was ten to now. Enough time to speak to Wyatt who'd just entered the room. Gray crossed over to her desk. He squatted down so he was obviously in her eyeline. But she ignored him. He coughed. Still she studiously went about her work.

Eventually he opened his mouth to speak.

"Don't apologise to me again," she said. "That's all you ever do."

Gray paused, the words stuck in his throat. Sorry was absolutely what he had been going to say.

"I wasn't planning to," he lied.

Wyatt put down her pen, turned in her seat, folded her hands in her lap. "Go on then," she challenged him. "I'm looking forward to this."

"I've tried to tell you several times."

"So this is my fault? It gets better and better!"

"I didn't mean it that way."

"What did you mean then, Sol?"

"If I could just tell you!"

"Well this is your opportunity!"

"Hope turned up totally out of the blue and she's pregnant."

"You're going to be a grandfather? Oh my God."

Gray winced at Wyatt's raised voice. "Christ, tell the world why don't you?" He glanced over his shoulder. Nobody seemed to have heard. Small mercies.

"I'm not sure I should be dating such an old man." Gray glared at Wyatt and she held her hands up in surrender. "Now *I'm* apologising."

"It's all been a hell of a surprise."

"Sounds like a huge understatement to me, Sol. What about the father?"

"He's keen but she doesn't want the child. Now do you get why I was being awkward?"

"Totally."

"All of this has been messing with my head."

"It's time, people." Yarrow in the doorway, beckoning everyone to his meeting.

"Let's talk about this later." Wyatt stood. "We'd better go." She walked past Gray. He got up as well, feeling the ache in his thighs from squatting for too long.

Yarrow, identically to yesterday, was standing at the front of the Incident Room. Hamson was nearby again as, of course, was Marsh, beaming his head off at anyone who was unfortunate enough to catch his eye.

When all were settled, Yarrow said, "Nearly time for you to go home, ladies and gentlemen, but not before I've made one more announcement." He smiled at the collective groan. "And that's for me to congratulate you all on your efforts today. The first Pivot operation has proven a huge success. We pulled in all but two of our targets. We uncovered valuable evidence at every property raided. Give yourselves a round of applause."

Yarrow clapped, quickly joined in by an enthusiastic Marsh. The rest of the team followed. Even Gray, though he rolled his eyes at Fowler in the process. When Yarrow had had enough he raised his hands, palms out. The noise quickly died away.

"In addition, we held parallel raids at a number of properties in London which we believe were undertaking County Lines operations straight into Thanet, led by DI Marcus Pennance. Some of you know him from previous work here last year. I'm also delighted to say these, too, were a sterling success.

"In total we've got thirty-one people downstairs, all of whom we expect to charge with a variety of offences. They'll be going away for at least a year, in some cases much more. DI Pennance and his team pulled in a further forty-three suspects in the capital. We got phones at every property, all with a series of numbers in them, meaning we can take down others in the chain – both suppliers and customers. We seized a total of 12kg of crack cocaine, heroin and Spice, with a street value of approximately £1.2 million. All in all, we've dealt the supply route a massive blow and there's a good chance it may never fully recover."

Marsh interrupted Yarrow, leading with another round of applause, though this one was brief, few of the officers bothering to join in, though he seemed not in the slightest embarrassed by his comparative failure.

"Thank you, Superintendent," said Yarrow. "Now, let's not kid ourselves here. There's going to be a lot of junkies walking the streets tonight, looking for their fix. That, in itself, is likely to lead to some problems. Also, we're all painfully aware from past experience that creating a vacuum simply sucks others in. However, for now we have some breathing space and plenty more scrotes to chase. Superintendent Marsh would like a word."

Marsh took Yarrow's space, the latter moving back a few feet to lean against the wall. Hamson nodded at her fellow officer, patted him on the shoulder.

"Really, DCI Yarrow has said everything pertinent. However, I'd like to single out one person for special mention. One man whose sterling efforts have made so much of this operation a success. Step forward, Sergeant Fowler." Fowler shook his head. "Come on, Mike. Don't be shy." Fowler's fellow officers parted, leaving a route for him to reach Marsh. He received a shove in the shoulder from somebody, propelling him on. Reluctantly, Fowler stood beside Marsh.

"Mike here personally identified a large proportion of the properties we targeted today. He worked long hours, undertaking surveillance and even making some deals to catch footage of the perpetrators." Marsh clapped for a third time, aiming his hands at Fowler. The rest of the team joined in, enthusiastic and not minding Fowler's special mention, because he had been working like a demon.

"However," said Marsh over the noise. "Mike failed to have one hundred per cent success, because one lot got away!" The team laughed, accompanied by Fowler. "But not to worry. For anyone who feels up for it, drinks are on me tonight next door at the Britannia." Marsh even got a small cheer. "I hope to see as many of you as possible." With that, the gathering broke up.

Hamson caught Gray's eye. "Wait," she mouthed. Gray paused while his colleagues threaded past him, Yarrow and Marsh included. Hamson stayed against the wall. When they were alone, Hamson pushed off, crossed the room and closed the door.

"How did your meeting with Marsh go?" asked Gray.

"I'm not supposed to discuss the details with you."

"Keeping secrets, Von?" Though Gray wasn't overly bothered.

"I'm telling you anyway. Marsh was wittering on about your acting inspector's position. He was asking whether Mike should be moved up to inspector, instead of you, based on his recent work with Pivot."

"If that's what Marsh wants, it's fine by me. I didn't look for a promotion in the first place."

"Well it's not fine with me, so I refused. I told Marsh you're the best man for the job. Because you are."

"You didn't need to stick your neck out for me."

"Marsh said it was my decision. However, Sol, knowing the Superintendent, it's simply a respite. He'll make the point again."

"Thanks, but why are you telling me this?"

"Because you should know what you're up against."

"You're assuming I care."

"I believe you do, Sol. Just don't screw up, okay?"

"You can rely on me."

"That's what I'm worried about. You're a good cop and you deserve to be an inspector. Anyway, I'll see you outside the court tomorrow."

"You're not going over to the pub?"

"I need some sleep. See you later."

Hamson left the room. Gray stayed behind for a few minutes, thinking about what she'd said. Maybe Fowler was a better man for the position. It was true; he'd done a hell of a job recently. Fowler had focused entirely on the task at hand in order to help him get over his marital and relationship troubles. Anyway, it wasn't Gray's decision who to promote. He followed in Hamson's wake.

"Should I be worried?" It was Wyatt, just outside the door in the corridor. "Spending time alone with your attractive boss."

"Just currying favour, you know how it is," said Gray.

"I'm going over with the Pivot team. What about you?"

"Just for one. The big day's tomorrow, but as Marsh is paying..."

"The enquiry into Carslake's suicide."

"I'm the star witness."

"I'd like to be there for you."

"That would look a bit strange."

"I know." Wyatt picked a piece of lint from Gray's jacket before leaning in and giving him a kiss.

GRAY DID LITERALLY stay for one. He made sure his beer ended up on Marsh's tab. When he was done he quietly slipped away, noticed by nobody except Wyatt. She waved as he departed, mouthed, "Good luck".

He turned the radio on as he left the station car park, listened to a couple of retired footballers as he drove, discussing a match which had been played earlier in the evening. It was bland and irrelevant in the scheme of things, which was just what Gray wanted.

Twenty minutes later he turned into the parking space beneath his apartment block. He drew up in his allocated spot, turned off the engine and headed to his flat.

Inside he found Hope sitting out on the balcony. She stood and enveloped him in a hug. "What's the matter?" he asked.

Hope released him. "It's Hamish; he keeps trying to call me."

"Have you spoken to him?"

"Not yet. He's sent me a text, though."

"What does he want?"

"For me to go back to Edinburgh. He thinks I'm making a terrible mistake."

"Perhaps if the two of you spoke?"

"I can't." Hope shook her head, in some mental vicious circle, unsure how to break out of the spiral. "Sorry, I'm just tired. I'm away to bed. Night, Dad."

Like when she was a little girl, if Hope didn't want to talk, it wasn't going to happen. Gray knew to wait for now. "Sleep well." She threw Gray a wan smile and headed off.

Later, when Gray was in bed too, he struggled to sleep, despite how drained he felt. The enquiry was looming large in his mind. He'd managed to keep the approaching date at a distance, focusing on the Oakley murder case and Pivot raids, but now it was imminent he could no longer ignore its existence.

And there was another milestone tomorrow. Gray was booked in to see his consultant, Dr Manesh, who'd been handling his cancer treatment. He heard Hope moving around, shifting in her bed. It seemed like both of them had thoughts weighing them down.

Nineteen

Then

The journey to Dartford had been easy, straight up the A2 in less than an hour and a half, keeping strictly to the speed limit. The roads were empty as it was nearing midnight. Fowler caught sight of the tight entrance for Vauxhall Place, between a charity shop and a bargain booze outlet, but he passed right by, carrying on along Lowfield Street. He wanted to cruise the area, check out the lie of the land. It was drizzling, his wipers squeaking as they wiped the water away.

It soon became obvious that this part of the London overspill was high-rise flats, run-down housing, shuttered-up shops. Kids on the street corners, despite the hour; dog shit on the pavements, cats running wild. Fowler drove past a social club and swung around; found Lowfield Street once more.

More like Lowlife Street, thought Fowler, though he hadn't spotted anything that made him want to delay the meeting.

He turned into Vauxhall Place. The lighting, already poor, dropped to virtually zero as he squeezed between the buildings, barely enough room to fit his car down. He drove slowly, twisting the wheel to avoid a pothole and potentially a broken suspension spring. He scanned left, then right, through high metal fences, the temporary kind that looked like they'd been there forever, given the amount of rust. A cracked sign strapped to one seemed to indicate the management company responsible, but Fowler bet they'd gone out of business some time ago.

Barely a couple of hundred yards along, the thoroughfare delivered Fowler into a courtyard which opened up to one side. His headlights reflected off a large puddle in the centre of a cracked cast-concrete floor, and beyond the graffiti-covered brick wall of a broken-down building. He could see a gap in the roof tiles, and plants growing from the gutter. A large bush was growing out of the brickwork.

And he wasn't alone. A Range Rover stood idling on the furthest side of the space, exhaust fumes spewing. Fowler halted, avoiding the puddle. A shaven-headed man got out of the car, came over, tapped on his window, pointed at the ignition and signalled for him to switch it off. Fowler recognised him for what he was. A cop. It was in the way he carried himself. The man pulled at the car's door handle as soon as the engine died. "Out," he said.

Fowler did as he was bid. Glass crunched underfoot, making him wonder what he'd driven over and whether his tyres were okay. He didn't fancy being stuck here at this time of night.

"Spread 'em," commanded the man. Fowler lifted his arms until they were parallel with the floor, like he was being crucified but without the wooden cross. As the man thoroughly patted him down, Fowler watched someone else in shadow soundlessly pulling a gate across the gap he'd just driven through, blocking it completely. The other man stayed in place, facing into the compound, ignorant of the rain. Fowler was trapped. His heart beat a little faster.

Search completed, the first man nodded Fowler towards the Range Rover. Fowler started walking, alone. As Fowler put his hand out for the door handle he glanced over his shoulder. Both men were watching him. He tugged, and the door popped, an overhead light brightening the interior. In the front sat a driver, only the back of his ginger-haired head visible. At the rear was Lewis Strang, immediately recognisable from the huge strawberry mark which covered half of his face. He wore a suit, tie and long black coat. It appeared to be on the way to a well-heeled function. Strang twisted his head so the blot was visible, daring Fowler to stare or make comment. Fowler ignored the bait.

"Get in," said Strang. "You're letting out all the heat."

Fowler slid his backside across unresisting leather; closed the door with a soft thud. The light went out a few moments later, though the compartment retained a muted light from the driver's dashboard.

"Would you like a drink?" asked Strang. He held up a small, metal flask. "It's green tea. Good for the circulation."

"I'm fine, thanks," said Fowler.

"I feel the cold easily." Strang unscrewed the cap, poured the steaming hot liquid into the cup. He took a sip. "Is this your first time in Dartford?" Strang made it sound as if they were discussing a holiday destination instead of the rough London suburb.

"I only ever go over the bridge." In fact, Fowler had done so yesterday. The Dartford Crossing, owned by a French company, all proceeds flowing out of the UK, arched over the Thames nearby, theoretically carrying thousands of cars a day, though it was often a long and expensive car park.

"I don't blame you," said Strang. "I grew up round here. Left as soon as I could."

Fowler didn't detect an accent. "Well done."

Strang leaned forward, tapped the driver once on the shoulder. "Off you go, Bob." Once Bob had left, Strang turned back to Fowler. "I hope your boss understands the scale of the favour I'm doing him."

Fowler noted Strang had made a statement, rather than asked a question.

"Jeff is aware of what he's asking."

"He'd better be. I'm here in this shitty place at a shitty time of night because I'd like you to impress upon Jeff that at some point I will expect something at least equal in return." Strang drank some more of the tea. "Jesus. Kids though. I really don't like getting my hands dirty with the underage. There's good money in it, apparently, but it feels wrong. Have you got offspring, Sergeant?"

"What's that got to do with anything?"

"To see if you understand."

"Jesus, Strang, can we just get on with it?"

Fowler felt a powerful grip on his leg just above the knee. Strang had one large hand digging in, the thumb finding a nerve. The pain intensified until Fowler cried out. Strang gave another squeeze before letting go. Fowler refrained from rubbing the area, which was numb and throbbed.

"This takes as long as I want, Mike." Fowler kept his mouth shut. Strang finished his tea, said, "Where is he?"

"Not here."

"What do you mean?"

"Change of plan."

"You surprise me, Mike. I'd heard you were smart. Messing me around usually has consequences."

"Hear me out. I've an alternative proposal for you. One which means you keep your hands clean."

"Interesting, go on."

"The kid isn't here. I've already dealt with him. So you don't need to."

"Yet here I am."

"My request is that none of this gets back to Carslake. As far as he's concerned, we met and the boy went to you. Therefore he's still in debt."

"Stitching up your boss, I like it. And I'll admit, not having to manage the child's disappearance is a happy occurrence for me."

"I'm glad we're agreed." Fowler put his hand on the door handle to leave.

"Not quite. It seems that you're asking me for a favour, Mike, yet offering nothing in return. There's not enough tipping the scales over to my side."

Fowler turned back to him. "What do you mean?" he asked, though knowing damn well what he wanted.

"I want your future loyalty as well."

Fowler had anticipated this, had already wrestled his conscience into submission. That Tom's life was worth throwing his own integrity away. "Two cops for the price of one."

"Three, if you count me." Strang smiled. He held out his hand. Fowler took it and shook. This time, Strang let Fowler get halfway out of the car before stopping him. "Mike." Fowler turned. Strang leaned over. "Give it five minutes before you leave."

The Range Rover drove off, pausing at the gate for the remaining man to open it up. He got into the rear. As he did so the interior light popped on and Fowler saw a pale shape at the rear window. It was Strang, staring back at Fowler. Then he was gone and the Range Rover disappeared up Vauxhall Place.

Fowler was left in darkness. He shivered, realising how cold it was. He returned to his car, got inside and started the engine. The wipers kicked in. A minute ticked by. A shadow fell across the windscreen. Fowler looked up. It was the tree growing out of the building, blowing in the wind. He couldn't wait here any longer. He put the car in gear and went slowly in the Range Rover's tracks.

At the junction with Lowfield Street he glanced up and down the road. Nothing and nobody. With a scuff of his rear tyres in mud, Fowler pulled away fast to start the return journey to Thanet.

Twenty

Now Gray tugged at his shirt collar while he waited. He felt hot, his palms damp, heat in his armpits. This was it, the moment when he learned whether six months of repetitive, bruising treatment had been worth it. The battering of his body with chemicals, allowing the cells to recover before repeating the assault all over again. The process had proved wearing, but Gray supposed that was the point.

The waiting room was a space located between the corridor and the office belonging to Dr Manesh. The area was functional. Beside the chairs was a table and some educational posters, yellowed in the sunlight. The wall paint was old and flaking, the light all unnatural – there weren't any windows. The room badly needed refreshing.

Gray heard the clack of heels on linoleum. Through the glass door, separating his space from the corridor, he watched two nurses in animated conversation walk past, one clutching a sheaf of folders to her chest.

Just behind them was Manesh. He entered, also carrying a folder. "Good morning, Solomon." He checked his watch, flicking his wrist so the white lab coat he wore rode up his arm to reveal the face. "You're early."

"Got a busy day ahead, doctor."

"Haven't we all. Please, after you." Manesh opened his office door and stood to one side, allowing Gray entrance. "And looking rather smart. All dressed up with somewhere to go?"

"An inquest." Gray had dug out his best suit and had it dry-cleaned in preparation. The smell of the chemicals was still on the fabric this morning when he'd removed the thin plastic wrap. "For work."

"Ah." Manesh was a good head shorter than Gray. His black hair was neatly combed and his small moustache precisely clipped. During their time together, Manesh had told Gray he came from Sri Lanka. Manesh's English was very good, with just the hint of an accent. Manesh had proved himself an adept and conscientious communicator. Throughout the treatment process, he'd explained each step concisely and listened to all Gray's concerns.

The doctor pointed at a chair before dropping the folder on a desk and seating himself. He pulled his chair in, smoothed his blue tie down and put his arms on the desk, covering the folder which he'd left closed.

"Let us cut to the chase, Solomon," said Manesh. "The delay in your care was a major worry for me."

During a case earlier in the year Gray had broken his treatment programme to focus on his work. Manesh had warned him of the potential consequences but Gray had chosen to ignore the doctor.

"I'm sorry about that," said Gray, "but it was necessary."

Manesh held up his hand. "Thankfully, it has not been a problem. I have good news, the best news, in fact." A broad grin split his round face. "I'm delighted to tell you that you are in remission!"

The relief burst through Gray like a tidal wave. He bent over, arms on his thighs. His heart beat faster. It was what he'd wanted to hear, but dared not hoped for. "That's fantastic."

"Isn't it? But let's be clear, I will need to see you periodically. Just to ensure the cancer has not returned. It is a scourge which has a habit of popping up again."

Gray sat upright. "Like whack-a-rat."

Manesh grinned again and pointed a finger at Gray, as if he was firing a gun. "Exactly that!" Manesh laughed. "Whack-a-rat, that is funny." Manesh stood and offered a hand to Gray. "Now go and enjoy your life and I will see you again in six months."

Gray got to his feet, gripped Manesh's hand and shook. "I can't thank you enough, Doctor." The words didn't sound sufficient to convey his gratitude.

Manesh waved his appreciation away. "Isn't it what we all do, Solomon? Look out for people? Especially those who can't for themselves?"

HAMSON SCUFFED THE butt against the wall, another black mark among many others.

She shivered, shoved her one exposed hand deep into the pocket of her knee-length black coat, and hunched her shoulders. She leaned against a thick wooden handrail the width of a floorboard, once painted white but little of the coating remained, exposing bare wood, grey with age. A few steps led up to the official building above, the Magistrate's court on Cecil Square in Margate, a short walk from the police station and on the edge of a busy road, the air tainted with exhaust fumes.

"How did it go?" asked Hamson.

"I got the all clear," said Gray.

"That's great news!" A motorbike sputtered past, the throaty exhaust's roar drawing Gray's eyes momentarily. "So why don't you look pleased?"

"I am, but it's all this, Von." Gray waved a hand at the edifice. The court building was an ugly, brick oblong with an appearance harking back to post-war modernism – all straight lines and angles, narrow windows and brutalist, which once would have been fashionable and now just appeared tired and over simplistic. A seagull, several feathers sticking out at unnatural angles, eyed Gray from the level above.

"It's good, Sol," said Hamson as she walked up the couple of steps to the entrance. "It means you can put everything behind you." Hamson dragged open the door and held it for him, the second time today someone had done that.

"True," lied Gray.

In the entrance lobby were a couple of security guards wearing black trousers, light blue shirts and dark ties. There were two walk-through metal detectors. Hamson handed over her bag before she went through the screening. One of the guards checked the contents, handing it back when she was through and he was satisfied. Gray passed the same guard his phone and wallet. There was a loud bleep when he set the sensors off though.

"Are you wearing a belt?" asked the guard.

"I am."

The guard held his hand out. Gray repeated the process, no sound this time. He took back his phone and wallet.

BURY THE BODIES 131

While Gray was threading his belt back on Hamson asked, "Which court are we in?"

Gray pulled the summons from an inside pocket and scanned it briefly. "Seven."

"Along here," pointed Hamson.

A small group was already assembled outside the closed door to Court Room Seven, waiting for proceedings to commence. Gray recognised Carslake's wife, Juliette, Jules to her friends, accompanied by her two grown-up children, Luke and Matthew. Even though he'd known she'd be here, he still felt a shock of guilt at her presence. She glanced at him, then looked away. He had tried to speak to her at her house shortly after Carslake's death, but the conversation had been terse.

Ben Clough, the pathologist, nodded at Gray. A few unfamiliar men in suits huddled together. They appeared to be reporters. The door opened. Out stepped the court usher, a woman in a formal skirt suit and white shirt, clutching a clipboard to her chest. She wore a name badge: 'Florence Vogel'.

"We're ready to begin," Vogel said, and stood to one side, allowing the attendees to file past.

The interior was as functional as Dr Manesh's waiting room. At the front was a raised bench, three chairs behind it and a coat of arms on the wall. The central chair, for the coroner herself, directly below the heraldic motif, was larger than those that braced it. Off to one side, and a row further forward, was the cube-shaped witness box, then three lines of tightly spaced seats butted right up to each other, giving little room for manoeuvre. Plain carpet, television mounted on one beige wall.

Towards the rear of the room was a further row of seats, split down the middle by a wide aisle. The small group Gray hadn't recognised made for the right-hand section, reserved for the press. So his guess had been correct. The opposite space was for the public. Anyone had a right to attend an inquest, but it seemed no one planned to today.

Juliette and her children were shown to the forward-most spaces, those kept for family. Matthew and Luke sat either side of Juliette. Gray, as a witness, was in the line behind with Clough and Hamson. Off to his left, Juliette's lawyer placed his briefcase on the table surface, clicked the catches and removed a folder. He put the case on the floor beside him.

Vogel, the court usher, hovered near the front, eventually announcing, "All rise". Everybody within the room stood when the coroner, Marian Lester, entered. Gray was aware, because he'd asked a lawyer years ago, of why the custom of standing occurred. He'd been told it was out of respect for the Queen, rather than the judge or coroner. Gray knew Lester. She was a part-time coroner; the rest of her time spent practising at her own firm, located here in Margate, off nearby Hawley Square.

She was in her fifties, well respected. Her hair was severely cut into a style shorter than Gray's. She had a scar on her face, just beside her mouth. Gray had no idea how she'd gained the wound. Lester was typically calm, no-nonsense and, above all, respectful to the families.

She glanced around the room and said, "By way of a brief explanation of process: we hold an inquest whenever there has been a sudden, unexpected death. These proceedings are not a court nor is anybody on trial. There can be no decision on any civil or criminal liability. Everything said in this room is being recorded. A transcript will be made available shortly after events are completed. This is merely a very limited enquiry into four questions. Who was the deceased? When, where and how did they die?

"As I am the coroner, I am in charge. I will call witnesses in order. When I do, they will move to the witness box," she pointed to the cube to her right, Gray's left, "where the usher will ask them to take the oath. Does anybody have any questions?"

Lester primarily directed her attention towards Juliette, but neither she nor anybody else responded.

"Therefore, I formally open the inquest into the death of Jeffrey Carslake." Gray noticed Juliette link hands with her sons. "I call the first witness, Dr Ben Clough."

Clough stood, walked past Juliette and paused before the usher, Vogel. She handed the pathologist a Bible which he held in his right hand. She then passed him a card and said, "Read this aloud, please."

"I swear by Almighty God that the evidence I shall give shall be the truth, the whole truth and nothing but the truth."

Clough relinquished the Bible and card and took to the witness box. He now faced inwards.

"Please state your name and position for the court, please," said Lester.

"Benjamin Whittaker Clough, Thanet District Pathologist."

"Mrs Carslake, do you have the pathologist's report with you?"

"We do," said her lawyer, responding on Juliette's behalf.

"You can leave at any time you wish, Mrs Carslake, if the evidence becomes too difficult," said Lester.

"I'll be fine," said Juliette. "I want to hear everything."

"Doctor Clough, can you confirm you carried out the identification and post mortem on the deceased?"

Clough twisted his head to respond directly to Lester. "I did."

"And can you confirm the body to be that of Jeffrey Carslake?"

"He was formally identified so by his wife, Juliette Carslake."

Juliette bowed her head. Gray imagined the process would have been a difficult one, given the way in which Carslake died.

"What was the conclusion of your post mortem assessment?"

"DCI Carslake was struck at moderate speed by a large object, which I understood to be a rollercoaster carriage. There were significant and extensive internal and external injuries as a result of what is effectively a blunt force trauma which occurred in the midriff." Clough pointed to his stomach and chest. "The force of the collision threw him several feet onto the ground where he struck his head, causing multiple fractures of the skull. However, I believe by this point DCI Carslake would already have been deceased as a result of the earlier impact. Death would have been almost instantaneous."

"Did anything strike you as unusual about the injuries?"

"Ordinarily I would have expected to observe damage lower down the body. Given the height of the carriage; at approximately waist height."

"What was your conclusion?"

"That DCI Carslake was falling as he was struck."

"Not lying down?"

"I would think not. Had DCI Carslake been prostrate at the point of collision then the wheels would have passed directly over him."

Juliette visibly flinched at Clough's matter-of-fact statement.

"Is there anything further you wish to add?"

"Not beyond what is already detailed in my report."

"Mrs Carslake, do you have any questions for Dr Clough?"

"No, ma'am."

"Then in that case, Dr Clough your testimony is sufficient for this court and you may stand down."

Clough returned to his spot beside Gray.

"The court calls Mrs Juliette Carslake to the stand."

Juliette rose to her feet and the swearing-in procedure was repeated. When she was in the witness box Juliette smoothed her dress and turned her attention to Lester, as if this were a discussion between just her and the coroner.

"Mrs Carslake, in order to ascertain the cause of your husband's death, the court would like to understand his mental state up to and including his final day. How did he seem to you?"

"A little quieter than normal," said Juliette, "but otherwise fine."

"What would constitute normal?"

Juliette shifted around. "Jeff was never a demonstrative man; he wasn't given to grand gestures and strong emotions. He was considerate and compassionate but he seemed a little more distracted than was typical when he was in the middle of a case."

"Investigations he was involved with would play on his mind, you mean?"

"Yes, how can they not? I'm sure Inspectors Hamson and Gray would say the same."

"I will ask," said Lester, "when their time comes. Did your husband ever discuss his cases with you?"

"Never." Juliette shook her head to emphasise the point. "Jeff tried his best not to bring his work home. He said he'd seen too many other marriages crumble because of it."

"But, despite his best efforts, the job would sometimes seep into your lives?"

"Not often."

"Was this one of those times?"

Juliette waited a moment before she said, "Yes."

"What case was he working on?"

"I don't know. As I said, he didn't mention specifics."

"What was his behaviour?"

"A little aloof, snappy, easy to anger."

"Did his conduct bother you?"

"Slightly, but we'd been married many years and gone through a lot. I thought it was a phase he'd eventually come out of when whatever he was focusing on was over."

"What was your reaction when you were informed your husband had died?"

Juliette paused, as if revisiting the memory. "Utter shock. Unbelievable really. It still is."

"You wouldn't expect your husband to be the kind of person who'd take their own life?"

"Absolutely not. He was a fighter."

"And since his passing have you become aware of anything which may have affected his state of mind?"

"It remains a complete mystery to me and my children."

"Do you have anything else you'd like to add, Mrs Carslake?" Juliette shook her head. "Then you may stand down. Thank you."

Juliette moved slowly, as if the weight of her ordeal rested heavily on her shoulders. Not meeting Gray's eye, she rejoined her sons, gripping their hands once more.

"The next witness is Yvonne Hamson," said the usher.

When Hamson was settled and procedure satisfied Lester asked, "You were present at the time of DCI Carslake's accident?"

"I arrived during the immediate aftermath."

"What did you observe?"

"Not much at first. I could see Detective Sergeant Gray, as he was at the time, near the rollercoaster ride. There were people screaming; others running away."

"How was DS Gray?"

"Calm. He was standing there."

"Did you find that odd?"

"I assumed he was in shock. He'd just witnessed the death of his oldest friend, after all."

Lester flicked at the notes in front of her. "In your statement you said there was a barrier restricting access to the ride and that DS Gray was outside the fence?"

"That's correct."

"And you found DCI Carslake's corpse beside the track?"

"We did."

"The other side of the barrier to DS Gray?"

"That's correct."

"How far away was DS Gray from the body?"

"Fifteen feet or so."

"Have you any reason to believe that DCI Carslake intended to take his own life?"

"I don't know what else could have happened. DS Gray was too far away to have influenced DCI Carslake's decision."

"He couldn't have stopped him?"

"As I've already stated, ma'am, I wasn't present at the actual moment of DCI Carslake's death but I struggle to see how DS Gray could have moved so far away by the time I arrived."

"You made mention that there might have been another person present."

"It's hard to say. There were lots of people running around at the time. I thought I saw somebody, a man by the look of it, near the track. But equally I could have been mistaken."

"When you say near the track, do you mean within the barrier?"

"Yes."

"Mrs Carslake, do you have any questions for DCI Hamson?"

"No, ma'am. I'm keeping my powder dry for one person."

Lester released Hamson then said, "Solomon Gray."

Gray stood, buttoned his jacket and made his way to judgement.

He took the oath to a God he didn't believe in, rendering the promise he had no intention of keeping.

To tell nothing but the truth.

Twenty-One

Now Juliette offered Gray a blank stare. Even with make-up her skin appeared pallid and wan, but her expression was one of grim determination.

"Please state your name and position for the court," said Lester.

"Solomon Gray, Acting Detective Inspector, Kent County Constabulary."

"DI Gray, you've been called because you were with DCI Carslake when he died. Please explain to the court the sequence of events which occurred leading up to DCI Carslake's death."

"I received a call from DCI Carslake. He asked me to come over to the amusement park as there was something he wanted to discuss. He sounded confused. I drove there as fast as I could, parked outside and entered. I found DCI Carslake by the foot of the rollercoaster. He was alone. We spoke briefly before, without warning, he moved in front of an oncoming carriage."

"What did your discussion concern?"

"He said he couldn't live with himself anymore."

"Why?"

"It's a question which has been on my mind ever since and I've still no idea what he meant. In fact I asked him what he was talking about. But he just smiled and the next thing..." Gray's voice trailed off.

"I've read your testimony, given shortly after the incident. You maintain DCI Carslake voluntarily stepped onto the track?"

"That's right."

Juliette shook her head vigorously.

"Yet Dr Clough's earlier testimony outlined that DCI Carslake was unlikely to have been upright at the moment of impact."

"He stumbled immediately prior to the carriage striking him."

"The court also has testimony from Sylvia Barrett, DCI Carslake's administrator. She said you burst into her office, looking for DCI Carslake."

"I did."

"She stated you were in a rage."

"That isn't true. Investigator Smits was present."

"Yet Investigator Smits and Miss Barrett declare opposing opinions. Why?"

"I've no idea, but Miss Barrett has never liked me."

"You and DCI Carslake were friends for many years?"

"That's correct."

"So you knew him well?"

"I thought so."

"What was DCI Carslake's state of mind immediately prior to the incident?"

"He was unhappy."

"Why?"

"I'm not sure. We'd drifted apart and didn't speak as much as we used to."

"For what reason?"

"He got tired of looking out for me. I'm not an easy person to manage."

"Would you say you're not a very well-liked man, DI Gray?"

"I've never seen my job as a popularity contest, ma'am."

"Do you believe he went to Dreamland, accompanying his grandchildren I might add, with the specific intent of killing himself?"

"I really don't know. I explained everything I was aware of at the time to my colleagues in my statement."

"You heard DCI Hamson comment that there may have been another person present near the track. Did you see anybody?"

"No, ma'am."

"Are you certain?"

"As much as I can be. DCI Hamson also stated there was mass confusion in the immediate aftermath, a view I concur with. And I was in a state of shock after seeing my friend die."

"You continue to believe that DCI Carslake committed suicide?"

"I do."

Lester nodded before turning to Juliette. "Mrs Carslake, do you have any questions for the witness?"

"Many, ma'am." Juliette gathered herself for a moment. This was the part Gray had expected and been dreading. He liked Juliette; she was one of the few people he'd got on with. He hated lying to her, but it was necessary. Gray was desperate to tell everyone what Carslake had really been. It was unlikely the full extent of his ex-friend's transgressions would ever come to light.

Carslake was dead and had caused massive damage while he was alive, damage Gray had to repair. And if that meant breaking the law to do so, he would. And if another outcome was sullying Carslake's name, so be it too. The man had done far worse than seemingly commit suicide. Outwardly, Gray had to show remorse, even though inwardly he loathed the man for letting him suffer all these years.

"Solomon," started Juliette. Gray forced his eyes onto hers. She paused, blinking back tears. "Solomon, we've known each other for a long time."

"Yes."

"Then for the sake of our friendship, and for yours with Jeff, I ask you to tell me one thing."

"If I can," said Gray and he meant it.

"What I want is the truth."

"We all do, Juliette."

"I just can't believe that Jeff would have killed himself. It would mean everything I knew about him would be wrong."

"I understand."

"Do you?"

"Completely." It was as if there was no one else present now, just Juliette and Gray, speaking with each other on a different level. "He was my closest friend."

"He was my husband, father to my children, confidante, my everything."

"I can't compete with that, Juliette."

"I'm not asking you to, Sol. I never have. But you saw a side to Jeff I never did. You were with him at work. Would you say he changed in the lead-up to his... to his death?"

Gray shifted in his seat. "He was different."

"How?"

Gray struggled for the words, even though he'd practised this in his mind many times. What to say, how to say it, to implicate Carslake and leave himself free. "It's difficult to express. He was... increasingly distant. Like he had something on his mind. Do you know what I mean?"

Juliette nodded, leaning forward onto her elbows. "Were you aware of his intentions?"

"No, and that's haunted me ever since. Could I have worked it out? Could I have stopped him?"

Juliette nodded again, tears running down her cheeks now. "And you're convinced he took his own life?" The words caught in her throat.

"I'm sorry, Juliette, I am."

She put her head in her hands and sobbed, comforted by her sons.

"Thank you, DI Gray," said Lester. "You may step down. The court will take a brief recess."

Lester rose, Gray not far behind her. He felt drained, hollowed out. As he passed by Juliette she dropped her hands, stood up and embraced Gray. She wept into his shoulder.

GRAY TOOK A WALK ALONG the seafront, hoping the fresh air would clear his head. It didn't.

He went into a café, sank two cups of tasteless coffee, then his phone rang. It was Hamson.

"How's it going?" asked Gray.

"We've taken another break. When Lester returns she's making her closing statement. I thought you'd want to know."

"I'm on my way."

Gray left cash on the table for the drinks. He walked quickly back to the court house and entered Court Seven just as the usher was pulling the door to. Hamson glanced over her shoulder. Gray nodded as he took a place in the public section to the rear.

Lester entered. When settled she said, "Based on the witness testimony it is the court's opinion that Detective Chief Inspector Jeffrey Carslake took his own life. It is also the court's opinion that he was under significant strain in the period leading up to his death and this contributed to his state of mind and led directly to his actions which he undertook solely at his own discretion."

Juliette Carslake sagged against one of her sons, her worst fears publicly confirmed. Everything she'd believed about her husband was wrong. Gray had no sympathy for Carslake, his legacy sullied now, but he felt sorry for Juliette and her sons. They had to live with the unanswered questions. Why had a husband and father taken his own life? Gray wasn't going to tell them it had been murder. One he could have stopped but didn't.

Lester continued, "Finally, I would like to take this opportunity to express the court's sympathy to Mrs Carslake regarding the tragic death that has brought us here today. I am aware how harrowing it has been for you." Juliette inclined her head.

Lester got to her feet. It was over. Gray had done it. Public record would state suicide instead of murder. But Gray wouldn't be celebrating.

Twenty-Two

Now Gray followed Hamson up to her office. "Happy with the outcome?" said Hamson when she sat down.

"Not really," lied Gray. "Just glad it's over." Which was the truth.

"We can all move on now. Speaking of which – the Oakley murder. Do you think our friend Parker has anything useful to say?"

Gray thought for a moment, having to change gears between the enquiry and the ongoing Oakley murder investigation. "Honestly? It's hard to be sure."

"If you were to take a punt on gut instinct?"

"Balance of probability is yes, he does. But Parker's not giving it up without a trade. Unless he voluntarily coughs we have no hold over him. Nunes is simply too unreliable."

"I spoke to Marsh about a deal for Parker. Marsh is prepared to make an offer, provided we successfully clear the murder off the books."

"What offer?"

"A good word to the judge, a much-reduced sentence in an open prison. He'd be out in a couple of years."

"Not bad."

"It's the best he'll get. Care to give it a go?"

"Right now."

"WHERE'S WORTHINGTON?" asked Gray. He looked around the Detectives' Office, not spotting the errant DC.

Fowler glanced up from his work. "He left ten minutes ago."

"Where to?"

"No idea."

Gray swore under his breath. "I wanted him with me while I interviewed Parker about the Oakley murder. Parker will be in front of a judge in a few hours so I haven't got long."

Fowler sat back in his chair with a grin. "Well, if it helps, I can fit you into my busy schedule."

"I'd appreciate it."

"Payment is expected, of course."

Gray knew Fowler too well not to have anticipated this. "How many?"

"Two."

"Two pints just to do your job?"

Fowler shrugged, "I'm seconded to Pivot, remember? This would be extra-curricular."

It was bullshit from Fowler, but that was the point. Gray sighed. "Okay."

"In that case I'm all yours for the duration."

Parker and his legal representative, Alfie Lakehurst, were already seated by the time Gray and Fowler entered. Parker, catching sight of the cops, turned his head away, refusing to meet Gray's eye. Gray took a chair, started the recording. Fowler placed himself back, out of Gray's eyeline.

"I wanted to revisit our conversation from yesterday regarding the murder of LaShaun Oakley," said Gray. Parker made no sign of having heard him. He tried again. "Mr Parker, yesterday you intimated you had knowledge regarding Oakley's death and you wanted to do a deal. I have a proposal. When your case comes to court, in exchange for information which leads to a successful conviction, the judge will take your goodwill into account during the sentencing process."

Lakehurst spoke up. "My client wants his charges dropped."

"I can't do that," said Gray.

"Then I ain't talking," said Parker.

"You need to give me something, Mr Parker. In exchange we inform the judge at your trial as to how much help you've been. Which should have a positive impact on your sentence. But I can't promise anything without knowledge of what information you have."

"Nothing."

"What was that, Mr Parker?"

"I don't know anything. I made it up. She made it up. Nunes was off her tits on drugs." Parker bent over the table, properly met Gray's eyes for the first time. "I know nothing, Mr Policeman."

"I think the interview is over," said Lakehurst.

"Seems you're right," said Gray. "I'll have you taken back to your cell, Mr Parker. Enjoy."

In the corridor, Gray shook his head in frustration. "I was convinced he had something to tell me."

"It was never going to happen, Sol," said Fowler. "I said he was pulling your chain. You still owe me the beer though. A pint a minute, that's a good deal." Fowler walked away. Gray went to find Hamson, to tell her another line of investigation into Oakley's murder was a bust. He was halfway up the stairs when his mobile rang.

"DI Gray? It's Alfie Lakehurst. Mr Parker's lawyer," he said by way of unnecessary explanation. "I'd like to meet."

"When?"

"Now. I'll be on the esplanade beneath the Winter Gardens."

"Very covert," said Gray. But Lakehurst had already gone.

Gray found Lakehurst where he said he'd be. The concrete esplanade, a sea defence, stretched along the coast, running into Margate one way and out to Cliftonville the other. The rear entrance to the Winter Gardens – a theatre popular with the stars decades ago, dug into the chalk cliffs – was behind him.

"Let's walk," said Lakehurst, turning away from Margate.

"What's going on, Mr Lakehurst?"

"Alfie is fine, now we're off-duty, so to speak." Lakehurst symbolically removed his tie.

"I'm still on duty."

"I can live with that, DI Gray."

"Solomon will do, if we're being informal."

"To answer your question, my client is scared for his life. He wants to help you, however, he's very concerned with regard to his safety."

"On what basis?"

"Something else he won't speak about. But yesterday, after the interview broke up, Mr Parker was very gung-ho. Today?" Lakehurst held up his hands in a query. "He's like a different person. He didn't want to even have the interview with you.

He'd have much preferred to stay in his cell. However, I persuaded him that it was best he told you on record that he couldn't help."

"Are you bargaining on his behalf?"

"Of course not, we shouldn't even be having this discussion."

"So why are we here, Alfie?"

"Duty of care, Solomon. Something bothers me about my client beyond being an alleged drug dealer, something I'm not comfortable ignoring should an incident befall him."

Gray stopped in his tracks, forcing Lakehurst to follow suit. "Spit it out."

Lakehurst shoved his hands in his pockets, hunched his shoulders. "Mr Parker believes he's going to die."

"Everyone dies eventually."

"But not by the hands of the police, Solomon. Mr Parker thinks one of you is going to shut him up. Permanently."

"Who?"

"I wish I knew. That's all I have. The rest I'll leave up to you."

Lakehurst walked back the way they'd come, ignoring Gray's call to return.

Twenty-Three

Now

The conversation with Lakehurst stayed with Gray while he walked back to the station. The accusation was sensitive. But who could Gray speak to? He was certain Lakehurst would deny making the allegation. And if one of Gray's colleagues had threatened Parker, the last thing Gray wanted to do was warn them that he was aware of Parker's quandary.

When Gray got back to the Detectives' Office, Worthington was at his desk. Gray made his way over. "Where did you get to earlier, Jerry? We were due to interview Parker."

Worthington frowned. "Sir? You asked me to get the CCTV footage on Harwood dealing. From Pivot."

"We haven't spoken about that."

"Not directly, no. It was DS Fowler. He told me you wanted it."

It was Gray's turn to be puzzled. "I said no such thing to him. When did he ask you?"

"A few minutes before the Parker interview was scheduled."

"Strange."

"Sorry, sir. I'd have been there otherwise."

"Not your fault."

"Can I interrupt?" It was Yarrow. "I hope you two are coming over to the pub with us?"

"When?"

"I sent round an email."

"I've barely been at my desk, sir. I've been distracted the last couple of days."

"I heard – the enquiry. But that's done, so even more reason to let your hair down. Everyone will be there."

A lightbulb went off in Gray's mind. "You're right. Of course, I'll be there. When?"

"Check your email." Yarrow grinned. "See you later on."

MOST OF GRAY'S COLLEAGUES were already in the Britannia when he headed along to the cells. Sergeant Morgan was behind a desk, tapping away at a keyboard.

Morgan paused in his work. "Not down the pub, Sol?"

"Heading over shortly," said Gray. "What about you?"

"Not my kind of thing, to be honest. Anything I can do for you?"

"Just wanted to ensure Parker had been shipped out."

"He went a few hours ago now. The judge saw him as a flight risk and refused bail."

"Where was he sent?"

Morgan tapped at the keyboard. "HMP Swaleside." The medium-security facility on Sheppey, about three quarters of an hour's drive from here towards London. "Is that it, Sol? Only, you're looking a bit shifty."

Gray forced out a laugh, which simply deepened Morgan's frown further. The Welshman was no fool. "Were you on rotation last night?" asked Gray.

"No, it was Finchley. I have that short straw this evening."

"Did anyone go and see Parker? Have a chat with him?"

"Now you're really making me wonder what you're up to."

"Just humour me."

Morgan checked the log. "Beyond the usual safety assessments, no. Parker was locked up tight all night."

"Okay, thanks. Time for that drink, I reckon."

"Enjoy."

Gray turned around and came out the way he'd entered. As he was leaving the custody suite, he caught sight of the CCTV. The lens was staring right at him. There was one outside the cells too. And the camera never lies. He decided to come back after celebrating with Yarrow.

"ABOUT BLOODY TIME!" shouted Yarrow as he saw Gray.

Yarrow was standing on a chair, raising himself a good three feet above everybody's heads. The whole pub turned and stared at him. Even for Gray, who was used to being the object of people's interest, it was a bit much. "I'd have been totally insulted if both you *and* your boss couldn't make it. There's a beer waiting at the bar. Somebody pass it to Sol! Now, where was I?"

"You're clearing off, at last," a heckler from within the throng shouted back.

"That's right!"

Gray got a tap on the shoulder. Fowler handed him a pint. Lager. He hated the stuff. Judging by the grin slapped across his face, Fowler had done it on purpose. "Cheers," said Fowler. Gray grunted in reply.

Yarrow was back in full flow. "As my erstwhile friend over there correctly said, we're packing up and leaving. As from the end of the week, you'll have your station back!" The crowd of onlookers cheered; even some who weren't cops. Yarrow was a good orator. "On behalf of us all, I'd like to say thank you for welcoming my team into your arms. Thank you for not bitching too much, and thank you for waving us goodbye tonight."

"We just want to make sure you piss off!" shouted the same heckler.

Yarrow raised his pint. "To you all!" He had a drink before stepping down from the chair.

"I'm going to miss this," said Fowler.

"Back to reality," said Gray. "With the rest of us."

"As Yarrow said the other day, there's still plenty work to be done."

Gray's phone rang. The number was blocked. He rejected it. The call came in again almost immediately.

"Are you going to get that?" asked Fowler.

"Could be anybody." Gray cancelled it. It rang once more.

"They're not taking no for an answer. I'll hold your pint."

Gray answered.

"Are you avoiding me, inspector?" Gray's hand squeezed the mobile tight. It was Duncan Usher. "Sounds like you're celebrating." Gray pushed his way through the crowd, getting outside as fast as he could.

"What do you want?"

"We need to talk."

"We are, right now."

"Face to face."

"Not going to happen." Gray allowed the silence to stretch. He'd been expecting this, that at some point his job would overlap with Usher's activities. Usher had taken longer than expected.

"All my routes to market are gone."

"Good, I'm pleased."

"You didn't inform me."

"Why would I? We're on opposite sides. Always have been, always will be."

"I could speak to your boss, tell her what happened at Dreamland."

Gray laughed. "You think you own me because of Carslake's death?" Usher didn't answer. "Let's run through the scenario. You roll up to the station, get an interview with Hamson and say what? Oh, Carslake actually didn't commit suicide as the enquiry ruled, it was me, I pushed him, and Solomon Gray just stood by."

"Something like that."

"You'd be locked up within seconds, confessing to a murder. This time there would be no way back. A life sentence would mean life this time."

"You'd go down with me."

"On what basis? Your word against mine? You'd lose twice over. Back in a cell and me throwing away the keys."

There was a long silence, Gray let it stretch. "I need your help," said Usher eventually. "I owe money, lots of it."

"Maybe they'll just take your hand. Isn't that what they do to thieves? Anyway, I'm having a drink with friends, I'd better be going. Best of luck."

"That's not how Strang works. He'll have me killed."

Gray paused, caught totally off guard. "Lewis Strang? What about him?"

But he didn't hear Usher's response. Something hit him on the back of the head. Hard. He saw a pair of shoes through blurred vision before he passed out.

Twenty-Four

Now Gray came to, something filling his mouth, partially blocking his throat. He tried to swallow, but couldn't. Tried shouting – all that came out was a muffled groan. He was gagged. Gray coughed, his heart pulsating. His head hurt where he'd been hit. Gray breathed deeply, in and out through his nose, trying to compel a tranquillity on his body that his mind didn't share.

When he'd calmed slightly, Gray lifted his face from the floor. His cheek was sticky. The air smelt of engine oil and there was dampness behind it. He looked around, waited for his eyes to adjust to the darkness and the spinning of his vision to settle. He couldn't see much, just faint shafts of illumination from above.

He attempted to stand but he was bound hand and foot. Legs tied at the ankles, arms in front. He struggled against his bonds but it was useless. His head began whirling again and he felt like being sick. If he did, the gag would block his airway and he'd choke to death. Gray stopped moving for a minute until he no longer felt as if he was going to throw up. He shuffled forwards until he met an obstruction only a few feet away. His fingertips felt roughness and damp, maybe bricks. Then he sat and stretched his legs out.

Brightness suddenly flowed through the cracks above. Footsteps approached, pausing directly above. He strained to listen. Without warning, the boards covering the hole were peeled back – two dead centre – lighting the interior further, making Gray blink.

When Gray's eyes had adjusted he recognised Frank McGavin, squatting down, staring at him. "Comfortable, Solomon?"

He couldn't answer, but McGavin knew that. McGavin shifted more of the boards until the gap was completely open. He glanced up, spoke to someone. "Get him out."

Dean Telfer stepped into view. Bald and stocky, dressed in scruffy denim jeans and jacket, a gold ring in one ear, followed by a young guy who Gray half recognised but his mind struggled to place. Mid-twenties, top-knot, side of his head shaved, cleft chin and a few piercings through his nose and bottom lip.

Telfer dropped the five feet or so to land beside Gray. McGavin and the younger man stayed up top. Telfer was stronger, much stronger, than he appeared. Between him and the young man they easily hauled Gray out. Gray lay on the ground, staring at the men's ankles. Telfer was wearing only one sock.

Gray realised he was in a garage. The hole he'd been in was an inspection pit. McGavin stood beside the shell of a car, rusting on its axles, an old-looking welding arc adjacent to it. Next to McGavin was a bench, a huge toolbox on wheels splayed open, the handle of a wrench visible, speckled brown. Nearby was a blowtorch which, in comparison, was unblemished. Overhead, strip lights ran in a line in the middle beneath the arch of a corrugated roof. One of the bulbs briefly flickered, but never lit up.

McGavin nodded at Telfer who pulled a knife from a pocket and opened up the blade with a solid snick. Gray fought hard not to piss his pants. Telfer sawed at Gray's bindings until they came apart, then stepped back.

"Get up," said McGavin. Gray rolled onto his knees and stood. He tugged the gag from his mouth. It was a sock. Probably Telfer's, given he was wearing only one. Gray bent over and threw up.

"Finished?" said McGavin. Gray wiped his mouth with the back of his hand. Telfer was smirking. McGavin pulled an office chair out from behind the car. "Sit."

McGavin patted the cushion. When Gray didn't move Telfer shoved him in the shoulder. Gray crossed the short distance and lowered himself down. McGavin was behind him now. Gray's skin itched as if ants were crawling over him. He wanted to turn around but resisted the near overwhelming urge.

"You can see yourselves out," said McGavin to Telfer and the young man. "And shut the door behind you. Don't want anyone hearing our conversation, do we, Sol? I'll call you back when we're done." Telfer left without as much as a backwards glance. The younger man gave Gray a long hard look before he followed in Telfer's footsteps. Three identical doors blocked off the wide entrance – one stood a few feet open, glass panes inset into the top quarter. Telfer closed the door, which moved soundlessly on well-oiled wheels.

"Ingham's a bit of a dick," said McGavin as he re-entered Gray's vision. He had to mean the younger man. "Fancies himself."

"Bit like you then," said Gray. He remembered where he'd seen Ingham now. Another one of Damian Parker's associates listed in the Pivot file. He was friends with Jason Harwood too.

"I'll give you that one," grinned McGavin. He went behind the car and dragged out another office chair. Duncan Usher was bound to this one. McGavin pushed the chair until Usher faced Gray. There were bruises on Usher's face, dried blood down his chin and his nose puffed up, purple and shapeless. His breathing was ragged. Usher turned his head, hawked up and spat at McGavin's feet.

McGavin crossed over to the workbench and began to search through a toolbox. He weighed a large spanner in his hand. Then he picked up the blowtorch before putting it down again. Finally, he opened a drawer and removed a sawn-off shotgun. He handled it briefly before placing it on the bench.

"What the fuck's all this, Frank?" Usher was attempting to sound tough, but Gray heard the quaver in his voice; saw him glance at the shotgun.

So did McGavin. "It's the changing of the guard." Ignoring Usher and turning to Gray, McGavin said, "You wouldn't know this place, Sol, but it's very familiar to me and my old friend here. We had a lot of fun here over the years, didn't we, Duncan?" Usher glared at McGavin. "We could do what we wanted and nobody knew. The old boy who ran it turned a blind eye. He passed on a couple of years ago and I haven't been back since. Until today. I feel quite nostalgic. In fact, this is where we were when Duncan received the call to tell him Valerie was dead. Duncan had just killed a man. Right where you're sitting, if my memory is correct." McGavin raised an eyebrow at Gray, as if daring him to comment, smiling when he didn't. "That's why he took the fall for Valerie's death, because he had to."

"Why are you telling me all this?" asked Gray.

"Just seems fitting." McGavin grinned again, clearly enjoying himself. "And it amuses me to know there's nothing you can do."

"Why, Frank?" said Usher.

"You've been away too long. You're soft, Duncan. Not when you were in prison. Only since you got out..." McGavin shook his head. "And when Carslake went, you became even more spineless. You know what disappoints me most?" McGavin waited for an answer. He didn't get one. "There's no fight left in you. The Duncan Usher I knew would be raging at me right now, straining to break those ropes, wanting to rip my throat out. But look at you. So meek. Such a pity. So, my old friend, there's only one use for you now. Everybody needs to know there's a new boss in town and, more importantly, they need to be totally aware what happened to the old one."

"What about my girls?"

"They'll barely notice you're gone, Duncan." McGavin turned to Gray. "And Sol, I bet you're wondering, 'Why me?'"

"Not really," said Gray. He attempted nonchalant, but it sounded forced.

"You stood to one side while Carslake was murdered by our mutual friend. I'm interested to see if you'll do so again." McGavin returned to the workbench and picked up the sawn-off. He reached into the still-open drawer and withdrew a cartridge.

As McGavin walked over to Gray he cracked the barrel, inserted the cartridge and closed it again with a loud snick. Mc-

Gavin held out the weapon to Gray. "Take it, blow Usher away and I'll be in *your* debt."

"Own me, you mean."

After a moment's thought, McGavin said, "I suppose that's right." He made the statement sound as if he'd not considered this option. "Well, as far as I'm concerned a man can never have too many cops in their pocket. And with Carslake's demise I'm one down."

Gray stayed where he was. "I'm not doing it."

"Meaning you don't mind someone else doing the dirty work, but you won't do it yourself?" McGavin brought the barrel to bear on Usher. Sweat beads ran down Usher's forehead.

McGavin laughed, lowered the gun. "Doesn't matter anyway, I've got proper killers in my entourage."

Gray took his chance, exploding out of his chair. He threw a fist, felt a connection with McGavin's jaw through his knuckles. McGavin rolled with the punch and swung the shotgun, catching Gray on the side of the head with the butt. Gray went down, face first in the dirt. His head swam. He froze when he felt the press of cold steel against his neck.

"Don't ever try that again." McGavin prodded the shotgun hard into Gray's neck then took it away. Slowly, Gray stood and turned around. "You've a good arm, I'll say that much." McGavin rubbed the area where Gray's fist had connected. He snapped the barrel open and removed the cartridge. McGavin got within a few inches of Gray's face then slid the shell into one of Gray's pockets then patted it through the cloth. "That's a reminder. Not to forget what happened just now."

McGavin stepped back, turned his head and let out a harsh, sharp whistle. Ingham pushed back two of the garage doors, creating a wide enough gap for a BMW SUV to reverse in, Telfer driving Usher's vehicle. Gray recognised the personal number plate. Telfer switched off the engine when he was a few feet away from Usher. Ingham pulled the doors shut once more. Telfer got out the car, left the door open before popping the boot. Telfer and Ingham got a roll of plastic sheeting from the rear of the garage and put it into the boot space.

"Sorted, boss," said Ingham.

"Looks like it's goodbye," said McGavin and threw the shotgun to Ingham, who snatched it neatly out of the air.

"You don't need to do this," said Usher.

"I know, but I'm going to." McGavin nodded. Ingham hit Telfer under the chin with the gun butt, catching Telfer and Gray off guard. Telfer sank to the floor without a groan, stunned.

Ingham and McGavin hauled the unconscious Telfer into the boot. Ingham went through Telfer's clothes and pulled out the lock knife. He opened the blade and plunged it into Telfer's torso once. Telfer, suddenly alert, clutched at Ingham's clothes, tried to pull himself up. Leaning in a little further, Ingham, ignoring Telfer's grip, put his hand over Telfer's mouth, muffling the screams as Ingham stabbed him over and over.

Gray had to get out. He ran towards the exit, expecting McGavin to stop him, but he made the doors and pulled them open. As he was squeezing through the small gap Gray looked back inside. McGavin was gazing at him while Ingham kept wielding the knife.

Outside, Gray immediately recognised where he was. The far end of Reading Street, the long, narrow thoroughfare which cut through this part of St Peters. A short run down the hill, where Callis Court Road became Elmwood Avenue, and he'd reach Joss Bay, a popular sandy beach hemmed in by high chalk cliffs. On a dark, clear night, the beam from North Foreland Lighthouse, the last manned lighthouse in the UK, would reach this far inland across the fields, filled with brassicas during spring and summer.

Gray turned right, away from the beach, half walking, half running in the direction of what there was of the village centre. He patted his pockets, his phone was gone but he had his warrant card and wallet. He needed to call a taxi.

The village pub, the White Swan, was close at hand. And they would have a phone. After five minutes of trotting and constantly glancing over his shoulder, expecting Ingham or McGavin to come after him, Gray reached the Swan.

He pulled the door open and tumbled inside. The place was largely empty. Swirly patterned carpet, old tables and chairs, fake black painted beams set into white walls in an attempt to make the building seem older than it was.

An old boy well into his seventies, from the generation when you wore a suit for most occasions, a ring of white hair encircling his otherwise bald head, was seated at the bar; the landlady behind it. They paused in their conversation and stared at Gray.

"Are you all right, love?" asked the landlady, her face split with concern.

"I need a phone," he said. "Police." He showed his warrant card.

"Behind here," said the landlady, lifting the hatch to allow him entrance. She was heavily tanned, wrinkled and wore a lot

BURY THE BODIES

of gold jewellery – fingers full of rings and multiple necklaces around her neck.

Gray lifted the receiver. "Can I get a whisky? A double."

"Course, love. Bells or Grouse for you?"

"Whichever."

She turned away, the rings clinking on glass.

Gray paused, debating whether to call Hamson. *I've just witnessed a murder.* It was right, but Gray simply saw a host of problems. McGavin would not let him off easily. That's why he'd taken Gray to the garage, to demonstrate his power.

The phone began to wail, too long off the hook. Gray got the dialling tone. He tapped in the number for a local taxi firm.

"Can I get a pick-up at the Swan, Reading Street?" asked Gray when they answered.

"Where to, mate?" asked the controller, a man.

"Broadstairs."

"Fifteen to twenty minutes okay, mate?"

"Can you get here any quicker?"

The controller sucked in his breath. "We're very busy, sorry, mate."

"Okay."

"What's your name, mate?"

"Gray." Being constantly called "mate" was becoming wearing.

"We'll get you sorted, don't you worry, mate."

"Thanks." Gray rang off.

The landlady passed Gray the whisky glass. He threw the alcohol down his throat in one. "Another," he said.

"Double again?" she asked.

Gray nodded. He took out his wallet, swapped cash for the booze, took the glass over to a table and sat. The chair was low to the ground, as if a good few inches had been taken off the legs. Gray swirled the whisky around the glass, staring into its depths, seeing nothing. Glancing up, he saw the landlady and her patron were openly staring at him. Gray realised he was covered in dirt from the garage floor, bruised and bleeding from being beaten. He stood, went to the bathroom at the rear of the bar, leaving his glass on the table.

Gray's reflection in a cracked mirror showed messed up hair and oil on one cheek. There was mud on his hands and knees too. No wonder they'd been gawking. He felt like pounding the mirror, smashing it into a thousand pieces the way he should have smashed McGavin's face. Gray knew he was trapped now. His moment of weakness at Dreamland had finally caught up with him.

Why had he thought he could get away with it? He'd known it would come back to bite him, that Usher would probably speak to McGavin eventually. Gray cursed himself for not mitigating the risk sooner. And he'd witnessed another murder. Could he have prevented it? The answer was no, and he'd have likely died himself had he tried. Gray knew the threat to him would extend to Hope – it always did. Family was a powerful lever. That couldn't be ignored.

Gray cleaned himself up as best he could; lukewarm air from the hand dryer removed the damp patches from his trousers. Standing on one foot and lifting his leg to get it close enough to the flow. While he dried off, it struck Gray that there was one person who could help.

When he was done, Gray went back out into the bar, his every movement watched by the landlady and her patron. Picking up his whisky, Gray drank it in three gulps. A clock on the wall told Gray there was up to another ten minutes before the taxi arrived. He couldn't stay here. With a nod of thanks to the landlady, he headed outside.

The Church of St Andrews was opposite. Hit by a sudden compulsion, Gray crossed the empty road and entered the place of worship. He took a pew at the rear. Gray felt inside his pocket, touched the shotgun cartridge. He withdrew his hand as if the metal were hot and burnt him. He bowed his head and prayed to a God he hadn't believed in for a long time.

Twenty-Five

Now

The taxi driver, a young man with a buzz cut and wearing a track suit left the Swan as Gray left the church. His car was bumped up the pavement, hazards blinking. "Are you Gray?" he asked.

"Yes."

"Control told me you be in the pub."

"Sorry."

"What's the address?"

Gray told him, then got in the back. The driver pulled away, heading the way he was already facing – back towards the garage.

"Can you turn around?" said Gray. "Go in the other direction?"

The driver frowned, not quite understanding. "This is the fastest route."

"Humour me, would you?"

The driver shrugged. "Okay, it's your money." He slowed to a stop, reversed into somebody's drive and returned the way he'd come. The journey would take five minutes longer, but Gray would avoid the garage. The taxi took a wide loop, eventually reaching Stone Road on the edge of Broadstairs.

Gray should have known this day was coming. Though he hated to admit it, McGavin had been right. Over the last few months, Gray had been lured into a false sense of security, believing Usher was content that justice had been done.

Gray had lost little sleep over his ex-friend's death. If it wasn't for Carslake, Tom would be home, Kate still alive, Hope would still have a family that she wanted to be part of. Carslake was in the past and Gray hated him now.

Stone Road ran near the cliff edge and that's how Gray felt – as if he was on the cusp of a precipice, ready to tumble into darkness. However, by the time the taxi reached his flat, a plan was forming in his mind.

As the car drew up, Gray said, "Can you wait here for me? I'll be back down shortly."

"Okay. The meter will be running."

Gray headed up to his flat. It was late now. Hope was in bed. Gray knocked on her door and entered. He flicked on the light. His daughter pushed herself into a sitting position.

"Dad?" Hope raised a hand to shield her eyes.

"You need to get up and pack."

"Why? What's going on?"

He squatted down beside her. She opened her mouth to ask him again. "Please, listen. We haven't much time. There's some stuff going on I have to deal with and you can't be here in case it goes wrong. Get out of bed, pull your things together. We'll be leaving soon."

"What for?"

"Hope, we have to go."

"You're not telling me anything."

"I can't. It's best you don't know. Please, get packed."

"I don't like this, Dad."

"I'm sorry, Hope. You have to come."

"What if I say no?"

"Then we're all in danger. The baby too."

Hope stared at Gray until she eventually said, "Okay."

Gray left a confused and scared Hope in her bedroom. He pulled the door to. The landline was in the living room. Before Gray placed a call, he changed his clothes, dumping his dirty suit on the floor. Next, he went into the bathroom and swallowed some painkillers, a mix of paracetamol and iboprufen, along with a glass of water. He dug a spare car key from a set of drawers in the living room. His car should still be parked outside the station.

He picked up the receiver, dialled Pennance. When the line connected Gray said, "Marcus, it's Sol. Look, I haven't much time, I need your help."

Twenty-Six

Then

As Fowler waited, he realised he was about to break the law again. He'd clocked off hours ago, told his wife he had to work overtime, but headed out for a couple of beers with some colleagues – to the Britannia, the pub next door to the station. So far, so usual.

When it was time to go he'd said to the lads that he was off home and, ignoring the boos from his friends, returned to his car. At the junction, he turned up the incline which was Fort Crescent, towards the Winter Gardens theatre, rather than take the road to his home. He entered the first side street and parked in shadow. After popping the boot, he retrieved a heavy carrier bag from inside and got walking.

A few hundred yards along near Trinity Square, Fowler found the phone box. Inside, the acidic stench of urine caught in the back of his nose. Fowler held his breath. The vandalism wouldn't take long. He removed a pair of pliers from the carrier bag and cut the cord to the handset. Job done, he headed back.

There was still time yet, so he took cover under a bus shelter – the legend, "Daz 4 Kaz" scrawled onto the plexiglass. The nearest lamplight was too weak to reveal his features to any but the nearest of passers-by. The bag was tucked behind his feet, under the seat. It was later than he'd thought, later than was planned, late enough that there would be no buses running now.

However, it was a pleasant night, the alcohol from earlier still delivering an agreeable buzz into his bloodstream. The cooling sea breeze dropped the temperature to a bearable level. Likewise, in the winter the same air currents warmed the land, keeping the frosts at bay. Opposite was a long line of terraced houses with magnificent views over the sea. Once private houses for the wealthy, now they were mainly given over to flats for immigrants or benefit seekers. But one was not.

The Sunset Guest House looked like its neighbours. Basement windows below pavement height, front door up several steps, then another three floors of plain, rendered frontage with inset sash windows. A sign in the window said "Vacancies". The light behind the curtains of this room was on; all the others switched off. Cars were parked bumper-to-bumper all along the road.

The guest house door was flung open and a young woman descended the steps fast. She dashed down the hill. Moments later a man and a much older woman arrived in the entrance.

"Rachel!" the man called several times. But the girl didn't stop. Soon the woman went back inside. The man waited several minutes, until it was clear the girl who'd shown her heels wasn't coming back. He retreated inside and the door closed. The road went back to its default, peaceful state. A couple of cars passed by in the following quarter of an hour, though that was all.

Fowler's backside was beginning to ache when he caught a furtive movement out of the corner of his eye. A lad, carrying a backpack was making his way along the street in fits and starts, moving like a rat in short, fast scuttles, using the shadows for cover. Fowler knew him. It was Regan Armitage, local troublemaker and the son of a wealthy property owner. Regan disappeared down an alley.

Fowler stood, grabbed the bag and looked both ways before crossing the road. When he reached the alley's mouth, he caught sight of a leg disappearing through a fence. Regan had entered the rear of the guest house. Seconds later, a cat shot through the same gap and dashed off in the opposite direction.

Fowler didn't have long to wait. A yellow light illuminated the wall above the garden. Regan squeezed out through the fence and followed in the cat's wake. He was heading for the phone box that Fowler broke earlier. Fowler entered the courtyard garden. The fire Regan had set was weak, the flames dying. More fuel was needed.

A fuel can and some oily rags came out of the bag. The man who owned the Sunset had a penchant for old motorbikes. A half-rebuilt machine rested at the furthest reach of the courtyard. Fowler kicked the stand, wheeled it over and reset it a few feet from the flames. He wet some rags with petrol from the can, threw them on the floor then poured fuel on the motorbike, splashed some towards the flames and dropped the can by the bike.

The fire caught, leapt high, making Fowler hurriedly step back. He was amazed at how quickly the blaze roared, climbing up the walls and leaping inside the house. Embers rose like fireflies. The heat was a caress on Fowler's face. He backed up further, mesmerised, until the glass in the kitchen window splintered then shattered. It wouldn't be long before the neighbours were alerted and the fire brigade called. Fowler stuck his head through the fence, glanced up and down the alley. It was empty. He stepped through and quickly walked away.

The Sunset Guest House was history.

Twenty-Seven

Now Gray checked his rear-view mirror for the umpteenth time. There weren't any cars behind him. If someone was following they were a long way back. His headlights lit up a blue sign with a white arrow pointing to the Medway Services. Gray didn't use the indicator. He slowed, pulled onto the exit. There were hardly any other vehicles in the car park. A couple of lorries nearest the building, there for the night, paying to use the facilities. Gray picked a spot close to the entrance. He turned off the engine.

"This is it," he said.

"What's going on, Dad?" Hope had barely spoken throughout the journey.

He twisted in his seat and took hold of Hope's hands in his. "We're going to meet somebody I'd like you to go and stay with. Away from Thanet."

"Who?"

"A friend. Marcus. He's police too."

"Why?"

"I need to be sure you're safe."

"What about you?"

"I'll be fine. Can you do this for me, Hope? Can you trust me?"

Eventually Hope replied, "Yes, Dad."

PENNANCE WASN'T HERE yet. Hope put her wheeled suitcase beside the table and sat down. Gray headed off to the counter to order a couple of drinks.

The service station was a long narrow rectangle either side of the dual carriageway of the M2, connected by a corridor like an extended railway carriage, the traffic running beneath. Floor-to-ceiling windows gave a view of the road itself – long and straight, originally laid by the Romans two thousand years ago. Within was a café, several shops, an amusement arcade and seating.

Gray carried a tray over with two cups of tea and a pair of granola bars on plates. He put the tray on the table, pulled out a chair and sat opposite Hope. A large vehicle whooshed past beneath them.

Gray kept glancing towards the entrance, but nobody came through the doors. "Have you heard from Hamish recently?" asked Gray.

She pulled a face. "He's tried to ring me a couple of times, but I rejected the calls. I'm still not sure what I'm going to do."

"So, you might keep the baby?"

"I don't know."

"What about finishing your degree?"

"It's not like I can't take the course again in the future." Hope shifted in her chair. "How long will this be for?"

"A few days, I'd think."

"Where will I be going?"

"London, probably."

"Why, Dad?"

"I'm getting closer to finding Tom." A pained expression crossed Hope's face. It was the first time her brother's name had been mentioned between them in more than a decade.

"Is that what this is all about?"

"Maybe." Truth was, he didn't know. He saw movement by the entrance. It was Pennance, pushing his way through the doors. "Ah, Marcus."

"You must be Hope," said Pennance. He remained standing.

"We haven't got time to waste," said Gray. "I suggest you get going." He stood. "I'll call when it's all over."

"Can I help at all, Sol?" asked Pennance.

"This is helping." Gray gave Hope a hug. "Everything will be okay." Hope nodded though she didn't seem convinced.

Pennance and Gray shook hands. "Thanks Marcus, I owe you."

"Stay lucky," said Pennance.

Gray stood at the window until he saw a pair of headlights swing onto the down ramp then take the M2 towards London. He was still there long after the tail lights had disappeared.

GRAY HAD JUST CROSSED into Thanet on the A299 dual carriageway when his phone rang. It was Hamson. He pulled over onto the hard shoulder, stuck the hazard lights on and answered. "What's up?" The clock said 4.01am. "We've a problem," said Hamson. "I need you here."

"Where's here?"

"The car park, underneath Arlington House. It'll be obvious when you arrive."

"Half an hour." Gray disconnected.

He could have a bloody good guess what would be awaiting him.

Twenty-Eight

Now The car park entrance, a gap in the concrete allowing access to a steep ramp which descended into a cavernous space, was blocked by blue-and-white-striped police tape and a pair of constables. Arlington House towered above. A few lights in the flats were on, even at this unholy hour. As Gray drew up, one of the constables stooped to peer into the car. Gray wound the window down. "You'll need to park over there, sir." The PC pointed. Gray reversed, found a space on the grass verge. He locked up, retraced his steps. The same constable lifted the tape to allow Gray to pass. He ducked under.

"Where's DCI Hamson?" asked Gray once he was on the other side.

"In the centre, sir. You can't miss her."

As Gray descended the down ramp, he spotted Hamson. Beyond the DCI were lines of cars. Hamson was with the pathologist, Clough, and both were in white evidence suits. crime scene investigators were crawling over the immediate area – only Clough and Hamson static. The Crime Scene Manager, Brian Blake, rotund in his get-up, stood in front of a white van, "CSI" printed on the side. Gray changed direction, made his way to Blake. Gray didn't like Blake much and the feeling was mutual. The moustachioed Blake leaned into the back of the van, and wordlessly handed over a suit, overshoes and gloves. While Gray was putting the gear on, Blake noted down his presence on the crime scene log, a piece of paper held in place by a clipboard, before he scuttled away, not looking back.

Suited and booted, Gray headed for the inner cordon where Hamson was waiting, standing on a square metal plate. There were more plates behind her, placed like stepping stones along the centre of the lane between rows of cars, their purpose to reduce impact on trace evidence at the scene. Hamson acknowledged him and walked on, indicating Gray to follow.

As he neared the end of the row he caught sight of a BMW SUV. He recognised the vehicle as Usher's. His heart began to thump. He knew what was coming. The plates led past the front of the car and around to the driver's side. It became obvious the interior of the car was a slaughterhouse. Blood and grey matter were splashed all over the passenger's window.

"Tell me what you see, Sol," said Hamson.

Gray took in the grisly tableau. A single corpse in the driver's seat, leaning over at an angle, held partially upright by the seat belt. It was Duncan Usher but Gray only knew because he recognised the clothes. Usher's face was gone; blown away, obliterated from close range by a smash of shotgun pellets.

Glass littered the floor and back seat; little irregular shards, mixed in with blood and brain spatter, and there were pellets embedded in the upholstery. Gray had been wrong, he'd only had a partial idea of what to expect. McGavin had outdone himself.

"He was shot where he sat," said Gray eventually. "From roughly here." Gray placed himself directly outside the driver's side. He mimicked holding a gun in both hands, aiming at the slumped body. "Obviously a shotgun, given the damage. The window was closed, fully or partially, when they fired. If I was going to make an educated guess it appears to be an execution. There's a statement being made by hitting him in the face. There has to be a purpose to it."

"Agreed," said Hamson.

"I assume we're looking at Duncan Usher? It's his car."

"We are." Hamson held out an evidence bag. "Found in his pocket."

A wallet, monogrammed in the bottom corner, initials in gold. "DU".

"No effort to conceal his identity."

"None."

"Where's Telfer? Usher rarely drove himself."

Hamson answered by leading Gray to the boot. She lifted it up. Inside was a huge sheet of plastic. Hamson peeled back a corner, revealing Telfer's wide-eyed stare. "Stabbed repeatedly."

"Jesus."

"Inseparable to the end."

"Has Clough given a time of death?"

"Nothing precise. He said we'll have to wait for the PM because of a concern he wouldn't voice. But we got an anonymous call about a gunshot just over an hour ago."

"No sightings of anyone fleeing the scene?"

"Of course not." Hamson snorted mirthlessly. "Frankly, this is all we need, given Pivot's underway."

"But we're done with that."

"So I thought. Wyatt will be staying in Thanet for the time being for continuity."

Gray frowned. "Is something wrong, Von?"

"I'll tell you later. I'd better call Marsh, give him an update. This will be all over the news. You know what this means, though?"

"What?" Gray didn't know much of anything right now.

"The coronation of Frank McGavin. The king is dead, long live the king."

Twenty-Nine

Now

The Major Incident room, recently reclaimed from the Pivot team, was in full swing. Whether the victim was a one or a ten on the arsehole scale, all murders received the same treatment. Maximum effort. No complaints, no grumbles. Everybody focused on what needed to be done.

But this was Duncan Usher. Gray's colleagues appeared pleased he was dead.

The Murder Board was being written up by Worthington. Two columns, for Usher and Telfer. Photos of the pair, before and after death, were being stuck up by another DC.

The phones were being worked. CID officers contacting informants for every shred of relevant information, no matter how seemingly insignificant. Likewise, uniform was out on the street, rousting contacts. All leave had been cancelled, every team member pulled in. For maximum effort, supposedly.

"Von," he said, keeping his voice down, even with the noise in the office. "I think you need to have a word with the team, remind them what they're here for."

"They should bloody well know."

"Are you sure, Ma'am?" Gray used the honorific deliberately. Hamson turned to him, frowning. "Two known criminals who half the team in here has been after for years are dead. And this is your first serious case in charge. You should stamp your authority on it, get everyone working in the direction you want, how you want it."

Hamson stared at him for a long moment, making him think his words hadn't penetrated. He was about to try again when she said, "You're right. Thanks, Sol. Get everyone together. We'll meet in fifteen minutes." She headed out of the Incident Room.

Gray spent a short few moments organising a case review. He found Hamson outside in the car park. At first he didn't see her, until he spotted the plume of smoke from around the corner. She was leaning against the wall, shoulders flat against the bricks, one leg bent at the knee

"Sorry," said Hamson. She dropped the cigarette and ground it out with the previously raised foot.

"A bit of cigarette smoke isn't going to start up the cancer again, Von."

"Nevertheless, bad habit." Hamson regained her earlier stance.

"No argument there. We're ready to go whenever you are." He mimicked Hamson, his hands behind his backside. He lapsed into silence, debating whether to talk with her about last night's events.

"You all right?" she asked, cutting into his thoughts.

"You mentioned Pivot earlier. What's going on?"

"Mike has been getting intel from his contacts that a new drugs supply has started up already. And it's proving very efficient, apparently."

"Yarrow did say it was a possibility."

"Agreed, but the minute the previous lines are gone? We were hoping for some respite. It's like we didn't put the slightest dent in the dealer network. Cheaper drugs and higher quality. As much as anybody wants. All from the one source."

"That doesn't make any sense," said Gray. "If you're the dominant supplier, why lower your prices? I'm no commercial expert, but isn't supply and demand a factor here? Lots of demand – constrained supply should mean higher cost, surely?"

"Mike thinks they're attempting to take a permanent stranglehold on the supply chain. Once they have all the customers in their pocket, they can charge what they like."

"It's almost as if they were ready and waiting for the competition to be taken out."

"Funny you say that, Sol, that's exactly what I was thinking." Hamson pushed off from the wall. "I've got to keep an eye on that problem so you'll be the senior investigating officer on the Usher case."

"Fine by me," lied Gray.

"Right, let's get back inside. You've two murders to solve."

HAMSON WAS THE LAST to be seated, placing herself at the head of the table. Not really her style, but it was the only remaining chair. Gray had arranged for the review to take place in one of the meeting spaces just off the Incident Room. Besides Hamson and Gray there were six others present, all from CID.

Hamson bowed her head for a moment. Gray knew her well enough to be aware that she was gathering her thoughts, but a few of the others threw glances at each other, wondering about the delay.

Eventually Hamson said, "I'm well aware the situation we find ourselves in right now is extraordinary. It would be easy to let the murders of two well-known criminals slide, to think that someone has done us all a massive favour. However, we are police. We cannot think that way.

"I would remind you that our primary purpose is to gather the facts and interpret them accordingly. It's far too early to know the why. DI Gray will be SIO as he has a long-standing knowledge of both victims. But remember, above all, keep an open mind. Carry on."

Hamson left the room, closing the door behind her.

"Okay, let's summarise," said Gray. For the next quarter of an hour the team ran over the crime scene photos and the information CSI had gathered to date.

"We need to generate more data," said Gray. "There's just not enough to go on. Jerry, get uniform knocking on doors nearby."

"Where, sir?" asked Worthington. "Most of them are commercial properties, shops mainly, so they're only occupied during the day."

"Somebody called in the shooting, and there are the flats immediately above the car park and a hotel across the road. Maybe they were outside having a smoke and saw something. Likewise with CCTV, drag off what you can from the nearby cameras. I want to know when Usher got into the car park and who arrived before and after him. Is anybody aware of when the PM is due?"

"Haven't heard, sir."

"I'll contact Clough. If there's nothing else, let's get to it. We'll reconvene in the afternoon to assess progress."

Gray headed to the Detectives' Office. There, lying in the centre of the desk, were his phone and car keys.

"Did anybody see who put these here?" asked Gray of everyone in the office. He raised the phone and keys up in the air. He received shrugs and shakes of the head in response.

One of Gray's colleagues had, though. He wondered who.

For now, that would have to wait. He wanted to know more about the man in McGavin's garage: Ingham. With a few clicks Gray pulled up the Pivot file on Damian Parker, the intel collected in advance of the raids. As Gray rightly recalled, Ingham, first name Richard, was outlined under the Known Associates section. The trio – Ingham, Parker and Harwood – had grown up together; gone to the same schools.

Next, Gray accessed the surveillance footage. There were several media files in the relevant directory. Gray played each one, watching them throughout. In all the segments Parker was outside, typically wandering the housing estate where he lived. There was Harwood, wandering the streets with Parker, buying something at the café where Parker worked, even heading inside the block of flats together. However, Harwood was nowhere nearby when Parker was dealing, which was why Pivot passed him over.

The final clip was the most interesting. Parker and Harwood were part of a group of five outside Staner Court. This time Ingham was present. In the background Harwood's girlfriend, Jackie Lycett, left the flats pushing a double buggy. Ingham watched her all the way over, while Harwood, oblivious, chatted to his mates. Lycett paused in front of the group, her back to the camera, trying to get Harwood's attention but he waved her away and walked off. Lycett gave him the finger.

The camera stayed on Parker, meaning Ingham also remained in shot. Ingham hung back briefly, putting his hand on Lycett's arm, leaning in, whispering something in her ear. Lycett recoiled, glancing in the direction Harwood had gone. She shook her head, walked away. Ingham watched her leave.

Gray sat back, considering the obvious conclusion. Ingham and Harwood knew each other and knew each other very well. It seemed as if Lycett and Ingham were involved somehow. And Gray remembered what Harwood had mumbled in the flat when he and Jackie were arguing while he was cuffed. That the baby wasn't his.

Gray rang Clough. When the pathologist answered, Gray said, "Ben, its Sol. I'm calling about the PM on Usher. What's your timing?"

"I'll be starting on him shortly."

"Good, I've got to be someplace else first, then I'll be with you."

"There's a risk you'll miss some of the operation."

Well, that was a shame.

Thirty

Now

Gray parked in the shadow of Staner Court, the high-rise on the Newington Estate where Jason Harwood lived. A few minutes later he was knocking on Harwood's door. It was opened by Jackie Lycett. She was dressed pretty much the same as when Gray had last seen her. Grey tracksuit bottoms and a stained Joy Division Unknown Pleasures T-shirt. Her hair was plaited. She looked tired.

"You again," said Lycett. "Jason's not here."

"Do you know when he'll be back?" Gray didn't mind. He'd rather speak with Lycett anyway.

Lycett shrugged. "I've got the kids to worry about. Jason can look after himself."

"Can I come in?"

After a roll of her eyes, Lycett backed away, leaving room for Gray to enter. He closed the door behind him.

"Kids are asleep," she said, "so we'll talk in the kitchen."

"No problem." Gray followed her along the corridor, past coats hung on the wall, boots and shoes beneath.

In the cramped kitchen, Lycett put just enough water in the kettle. "Want a coffee?" she asked.

"I'm good, thanks."

Kettle on, Lycett reached into cupboards, grabbed a mug from one, a jar of instant from another. The work surfaces were crammed with baby gear. A large tub filled with bottles and teats, sterilising for future use, containers of baby-milk powder. The sink was a jumble of dirty crockery. The view out the window was over Ramsgate rooftops.

"What do you want?" asked Lycett after she'd made her drink. She held the steaming mug and leaned against the sink, the light from the window behind creating an aura around her.

"Ray Ingham."

Lycett's hand shook. She put the mug down. "What about him?"

"How well do you know him?"

"What does that mean?"

"Does he come here often?"

"Every now and again, he's one of Jason's mates."

"Always when your boyfriend is here?" Lycett didn't answer. She picked the mug up – took a sip.

"When I was searching the flat the other day, Jason said something interesting. That the baby wasn't his. Whose is it, Jackie?"

She dropped the mug. It burst into pieces on the floor, spraying ceramic shards and hot coffee everywhere. "Get out." She pushed off the sink, pointed at the door. "Get out!"

Gray stood. "You two want to be together but Jason is in your way and Ray decided to fix the problem. Is that it?"

Lycett turned, picked up a food-encrusted plate and hurled it in his direction. Gray ducked and the plate shattered against the wall. As Lycett picked up a bowl, he ran into the corridor. The bowl broke a few feet from him. He reached the front door, Lycett following, a knife in her hand. She shrieked, "You bastard!"

As Gray opened the door, the baby began to cry. Lycett paused, torn between chasing Gray and attending to her offspring. Gray took his chance and bolted, slamming the door behind him. Rather than wait for the lift he took the stairs.

Gray was panting by the time he reached the ground floor. Lycett hadn't pursued him. He headed out to the car, digging his keys and his mobile out of his pocket as he walked. A huge smash beside him made Gray leap sideways. A plant pot had hit the ground, spraying soil and leaves everywhere. He looked up. Lycett was leaning over a railing, an object raised above her head; a deck chair. She let go. Gray watched its trajectory and dodged it. Lycett backed away and Gray got into his car.

When he was a safe distance away, he called Worthington. "Jerry, I'm at Staner Court. Harwood's girlfriend has gone off on one. Started chucking stuff at me. Get uniform down here so we can pull her in."

"I'll see where the nearest car is, sir."

"Call Social Services too. The kids are with her."

"Will do." Worthington rang off.

Within three minutes a squad car, lights flashing, entered the grounds of Staner Court. It hadn't taken long because there was always a patrol around the Newington Estate; visible policing. The two uniforms got out.

"Anybody else on their way?" asked Gray.

One of the constables, a grizzled veteran known in the station as Gripper, eyed the plant pot. "Just behind us, Sol. A bit of gardening gone wrong?"

Gray was glad it was Gripper; he was a big bastard with a busted nose and small eyes. He could cow people just by looking at them. Before Gray could answer, a second car arrived, spilling out two more officers. Gray explained the situation.

"Should be more than enough," said Gripper when Gray had finished. "Let's get this done then."

The door to Harwood's flat was closed. Gray tried the handle. It was locked. Gray knocked, shouted, "Jackie, it's Inspector Gray. Open up please." No answer. He hammered on the door again. Still no response.

"Want me to break it down?" asked Gripper.

"Go ahead," said Gray.

Gripper stepped back, raised a foot and kicked out, his boot hitting the door just above the handle. The wood cracked. Gripper shouldered the door open.

Gray entered, closely followed by Gripper. "Jackie," said Gray. "Let's sort everything out." Lycett didn't answer. Gray made his way slowly along the corridor, alert. He found Lycett on the balcony. She was sitting on the railing, the baby in her arms. If she moved her weight at all she and the baby would fall. Gray remained in the doorway. He motioned for Gripper to stay back.

"Jackie," said Gray. "Come inside and let's talk." Gray took a slow step forward.

"You won't listen to me," said Lycett.

"I'm here now." Gray moved further towards Lycett. She watched him, but didn't protest. "Tell me whatever you want."

"They'll take my kids."

"You don't know that."

Lycett looked away from Gray and down at the drop beneath. Gray got to six feet away from her. "No closer," said Lycett. The baby began to cry. Lycett rocked her gently.

"I've a daughter too," said Gray. "There's nothing more important to me than her. Jackie, this isn't the answer."

"What's she called, your daughter?"

"Hope. She's pregnant. I'm going to be a grandfather soon." He shuffled further a little more. Gray was within reaching distance. "Please come down and we'll talk about it. I promise we'll do right by you and your children."

"I don't believe you." Jackie closed her eyes and began to tip backwards. Gray leapt forward and got a hold of Jackie's arm. She shrieked, Gray's grip making her twist so she was facing down. The baby began to wail. Gray hung on, fighting gravity while Jackie struggled. Then Gripper was beside Gray. Between them they hauled Jackie off the railing. She collapsed to the floor, hugging the baby to her chest.

"Christ, that was close," said Gripper.

GRAY HAD TO AWAIT THE arrival of Social Services, so by the time he negotiated his way to the Queen Elizabeth The Queen Mother Hospital on the edge of Margate, parked and found the post-mortem suite, the analyses were already underway. The corpse's head was nearest Gray. Clough had just opened up the brain cavity. Gray couldn't tell if this was Telfer or Usher.

Clough was bent over the body in the examination room itself, all white tiles and stainless steel, dazzling spotlights, glittering surgical instruments, and gaping drains, everything designed for an easy clean.

The viewing area was separated from Clough's workspace by a large plate-glass window. It was plain in comparison, as if the lion's share of the budget had been reserved for the dead. The walls were washed in a lemon yellow; rows of uncomfortable chairs fixed to the floor, all facing the same direction – towards the window. The spectacle of evisceration was difficult to avoid. The air was icy and stank of disinfectant. Gray kept his coat on and breathed through his mouth.

The pathologist must have caught Gray's movement because he looked up from his work. Clough was dressed in a lab coat, pure white. He wore purple nitrile gloves and a mask across the lower half of his face. His hair was beneath a cap so just a thin strip between his brow and the bridge of his nose was visible.

Clough flicked a switch. "Nice to see you, Sol," he said. Gray raised a thumb in response. The communication was one way. "Mr Telfer has been dealt with; I'm just with Mr Usher at the moment. Shouldn't be long. I'm almost through."

Gray had to admit he was pleased he wouldn't be witnessing much of the evisceration. It was a procedure he would never get used to and never wanted to.

"I should be no more than thirty minutes," said Clough, clicking off the intercom, meaning Gray wouldn't be listening to the pathologist's running commentary.

In fact, Clough required less than time than he said, during which Gray attempted to look anywhere else but through the glass. At times he wished he still smoked, the perfect opportunity to go outside. Gray fiddled with his phone instead. Clough would understand.

Clough finally said, "I'm done." The pathologist, keeping bloodied hands raised, pushed his way through a pair of double doors to the rear. He would be cleaning down now, stripping off his gear.

Gray, glad to exit, headed for Clough's office, a tiny affair, barely enough room for a desk with a chair, and two more for visitors. For a tall person like Gray, sitting down meant his knees were pretty much pushed up to the desk itself. On the back wall were a couple of framed diplomas. A bookcase to Gray's right held medical journals. Light entered through windows inset with chicken wire the size and shape of graph paper.

It took Clough a couple of minutes to clean down. He shouldered the door, having to close it first before he could access his chair. Clough shook hands with Gray and flopped down in his seat. As usual, the pathologist's palms were as cold as melting ice.

"Can't keep away it seems, Sol."

"It's all the dying people," said Gray. Clough snorted in his approximation of a laugh. "Initial thoughts?"

"First, I concur with the scene-of-crime officers that the weapon used to kill Mr Usher was a shotgun." Clough paused, pointed past Gray. "Pass me that book, would you, Sol?"

Gray handed Clough the volume he wanted. The pathologist riffled through until he hit the right section. Gray stood up to see what Clough was looking at; a series of photos of damaged corpses.

"This is an article by a man called Cassidy who spent a lot of time analysing shotgun wounds."

"Lucky guy." Gray returned to his seat.

"Quite. Now, I have to compare the images I took during the PM with these. If there is up to a metre between shooter and victim, the central wounds are still in the region of two-

and-a-half to four centimetres in diameter. When the shooter is more than a metre away, scalloping of the wound is observed." Clough flipped through the book, settling on another section further through. "Unlike rifles, shotguns don't generally lead to exit wounds unless there's a contact wound to the head.

"Which means that if the barrel was touching the head when fired, I'd expect to see massive destruction because the combustion gases produced during the firing also enter the skull. Their expansion would have blown Usher's cranium apart, spreading bone and skin fragments far and wide. I'd only be able to determine the exact point of entry via a painstaking reconstruction by literally piecing bone fragments together like a grisly jigsaw. Also, there would be soot, burn and carbon marks and unburnt powder." Clough closed the textbook.

"I conclude that Mr Usher was killed by a single blast from an intermediate velocity shotgun removing most of his face and the back of his head. From the amount of damage and the lack of secondary materials I'd say he was shot from around a metre or so. Death would have been instantaneous and occurred an hour previous to my arrival at the scene, approximately 3am. I'd say he definitely died in the car."

"There's a but," said Gray, because he knew there was. "Right?"

"Yes. Can you put this back please?" Clough handed Gray the book. Clough continued. "I found ligature marks on his wrists and ankles, sufficiently deep to suggest he'd been tied up for a period of time beforehand. And they were very recent."

"I'll see whether CSI found any rope in the car. What about Telfer?"

"Yet another interesting conundrum, Sol. He was wrapped in a large sheet of plastic. His blood had pooled within the sheet. I also found blood had settled along the back of his body so I surmise he was stabbed to death in-situ. The amount of pooling would indicate a time of death earlier than that of Mr Usher by a good four to five hours."

"Had he been bound as well?" Again, Gray knew the answer but needed to go through the motions.

"There weren't any indications of restraint, no."

"Okay."

"If that's all, I'll write up my report forthwith."

"Thanks, Ben," said Gray.

Gray left Clough to his writing and headed back to his car. When he arrived at the station he went straight up to Hamson.

"I've just been to Usher and Telfer's PMs," said Gray. "Time of death differed between the two of them. Telfer around 10 or 11pm, Usher approximately 3am. Both were murdered in the car, but Usher had been bound for a period beforehand."

"Bound?" asked Hamson.

"That's right. I need to check if there was any rope in CSI's manifest."

"We can see now. Just a moment."

Hamson tapped away at her keyboard to access the electronic file. "No, nothing even close to a binding."

"Based on Clough's findings, and the first report of the shooting coming in, it's reasonable to assume that Telfer was already dead by the time Usher arrived. The question is whether Usher drove himself or if somebody else did."

"We need CCTV to help make sense of this."

"Agreed."

"What about McGavin?" asked Hamson. "You'll be interviewing him at some point? As Usher was his business partner and mentor."

"I doubt we'll learn anything from him."

"His attitude will be interesting though. What do you reckon, happy or sad?"

"When it comes to McGavin, guessing is futile."

Thirty-One

Now

Gray was on the verge of entering the Detectives' Office when Wyatt caught him. "You look dreadful, Sol. Are you all right?"

"It's all these early starts. They're beginning to catch up with me."

"I guess you heard the intel? About the new drugs supply?"

"Yvonne told me earlier."

"It's awful, though I suppose every cloud has a silver lining. I get to stay here a little longer."

"Not under the best of circumstances, Emily."

"You don't want me around then, inspector?"

"That isn't how I meant it to come out."

"I'm just joking, Sol. God, where's your sense of humour?"

"In bed. What's the latest?"

"I'm still trying to untangle what's happening out on the streets. Mike has been putting the hours in talking to his contacts. But what's obvious is there's a new, better supply which is going down a storm and definitely a replacement line out of London. They're clearing up. Desperate customers, pristine product at a lower price. If you're a junkie, what's not to love?"

"What does Yarrow think?"

"He's got Sheerness in his targets now. Speaking of which, a friend of mine has been trying to reach you."

"Who?"

"Elise Trent, the governor at HMP Swaleside. I met her on an Open University course a few years ago. We got on really well and we've stayed in touch since."

Gray frowned. "Swaleside is where Parker got sent on remand."

"If you say so. Anyway, she's been trying to call and couldn't reach you and asked me to pass on her number. She seemed pretty pissed off." Wyatt handed over a scrap of paper as her mobile jingled.

"Pissed off?" asked Gray. "Why?"

"It's Mike," said Wyatt checking the phone's screen. "Sorry, I'd better take this. I'll see you later."

Gray stared at the paper as Wyatt drifted away but he was only going to learn what Trent wanted by calling her. She answered within a couple of rings.

"Miss Trent, Inspector Gray returning your call."

"Ah! The elusive policeman. I've tried to contact you several times. I even left a voicemail."

"Sorry, this is the first I knew about it."

"I rang on this number, I assure you."

"I don't know what went wrong."

"Most recently the call wouldn't connect. It was as if I'd been blocked from doing so."

"Not by me. Anyway, how can I help?"

"I'm afraid this is all after the event."

"I don't understand, Miss Trent."

"Mr Parker wanted to speak to you; he was very animated about it."

"Why?"

"He wouldn't tell me, but he was extremely concerned for his safety, kept insisting his life was in danger."

"Who from?"

"He wouldn't say. However, he was proved correct. Mr Parker was stabbed this morning by another inmate while he waited in a queue for breakfast. He's in a critical but stable condition in hospital."

"Jesus. Is he going to make it?"

"Touch and go, inspector. It's been chaos here since."

"I'm not surprised. Why was he attacked?"

"He's not in any fit state to talk right now and I doubt he'll do so when he wakes. Nobody wants to be known as a grass."

"What do you think?"

"It's a puzzle. I don't know Parker and his assailant hasn't been violent previously."

"Is he saying anything about why he went for Parker?"

"Not a word, despite the prospect of a lengthened custodial sentence. I'm sorry there's not much more I can tell you."

"Thanks for letting me know."

"I'm just sorry it isn't better news."

"Could you keep me appraised of his situation?"

"Of course."

Gray ended the call and headed back to his desk. He considered what Trent had told him. All Gray could think of was that Parker had some information he was prepared to share. And what was the motive for his attempted murder? To keep him quiet? Gray checked his phone logs. The screen was blank, no missed calls. Next he checked his voicemail, that was empty too.

There was one occasion Gray had been without his mobile. In McGavin's garage. And the phone had turned up on Gray's desk, with his car keys. So somebody had put them there. Gray hadn't had a chance to consider this, given the recent rapid-fire events. Perhaps the calls had been deleted?

However, if his log had been wiped there were other ways he could find out the activity. The police had automated access to the largest phone providers via UFED, a piece of data analysis kit manufactured by an Israeli company called Cellebrite. The Public Protection Unit used the machines as standard to check the phones owned by suspected sex offenders. Think a secure password or erasing the phone's memory was sufficient to protect you from prying eyes? Think again. Not even smashing the phone to pieces these days worked if the memory chips were recovered in one piece.

The PPU was on the other side of the building. Gray knew one of the inspectors back from when he used to smoke. It was amazing who you could get talking to outside over a burning ember.

WHEN GRAY WALKED INTO the PPU he received the merest of glances from the team working away. Gray couldn't see his erstwhile smoking buddy, Inspector Karsten Albrecht, a German by birth.

"Anyone seen Karsten?" asked Gray.

"He left a few minutes ago. I'm sure he'll be back soon," said a woman next to Gray. "Can I help?"

"I'll find him, thanks."

Gray went outside and, as expected, found Albrecht finishing up a cigarette. "I thought you'd given up, Sol." Albrecht had lived in the UK for more than a decade. He wore large, black-rimmed glasses and sported a close-trimmed goatee. Albrecht extracted another cigarette and offered Gray the packet.

"I have." Gray took the unlit cigarette from Albrecht's lips. "I'm after your help."

"Now?"

"I'm sure a man of your expertise won't take long." Gray handed Albrecht the cigarette and the German slid it back into the packet with a shrug.

"Flatterer. What is it you need?"

"A phone looking at."

"Whose?"

"Confidentially?"

"Of course."

"Mine."

Albrecht raised an eyebrow. "Interesting."

At a table in the centre of the office space sat the black box. It wasn't much larger than a mobile, square and squat with an LED readout and four buttons, each with an arrow pointing up, down, left and right for navigation purposes. Cables ran from the UFED system to a computer. Gray handed Albrecht his phone. Albrecht plugged the unit into UFED via a standard USB connection.

"What specifically do you want?" asked Albrecht.

"A list of the calls from the last three days."

"Easy," said Albrecht, "just give me a moment." Albrecht used the arrows to scroll through the system options. "Here you go." The incoming and outgoing calls came up on the screen as a list. Time, date and length.

"Can I get a hard copy?"

"Sure." A couple of clicks on a mouse and a printer whirred nearby. Albrecht collected them and handed over two sheets of paper to Gray. "Is that it?"

"Told you it would be fast. Drinks are on me next time we're out," said Gray.

Albrecht raised a hand in protest. "You owe me nothing. It was straightforward." He went to disconnect the phone.

Something occurred to Gray. "Actually, one other thing. Can you retrieve deleted voicemails?"

"Within the same timeframe?"

Gray nodded. Albrecht went back to UFED and tapped away. Moments later, Albrecht looked over his shoulder and said, "Want to hear it now?"

"Please."

Albrecht clicked the mouse. On the monitor a window popped up with a pattern like a voice print. Another click, and Trent's voice issued over the speakers in time with a band moving along the print.

"Hello, Inspector Gray, this is Elise Trent from HMP Swaleside. Could you give me a ring back, please?" She then read out her mobile number.

"Okay?" asked Albrecht.

"Perfect."

"Do you want the message as an audio file? I can email it over."

"That would be great. And I'm definitely done now." He shook Albrecht's hand. "I appreciate it."

"Any time."

Back at his desk there was a steaming cup awaiting him. Fowler sitting nearby, raised a mug and said, "Thought I'd make you one for a change."

"Thanks."

Gray compared the printout against the piece of paper with Trent's details. Three calls from the mobile and another from a landline. A quick internet search confirmed the dialling code was that of nearby Sheerness. It was a good bet this would be Trent also. So somebody had intercepted and dealt with them, maybe after hearing Trent's voicemail. It had to be McGavin.

Gray thought back to his last interview with Parker; how he'd been evasive. The discussion had been recorded on CCTV and Gray could review the footage from where he sat because everything was stored on a central server. With a few clicks, the tape was playing. The perspective was from on high, the camera mounted on the wall above the table and pointing down in order to best observe the subject.

Parker was furtive, his behaviour almost the polar opposite of the previous day. At the time, Gray had thought Parker wouldn't meet his eye, but as he watched afresh he changed his opinion. It wasn't Gray that Parker was avoiding, but Fowler.

Gray also recalled the camera in the corridor outside the cells. He could access that too. He went back a couple of days, watched Parker being installed in his cell by Sergeant Morgan, the door being locked, Morgan turning and walking away. Gray spooled forwards at 16x speed, slowing down whenever anybody went near Parker's door. Several times Morgan checked on Parker, peering in through the peephole, giving Parker a tray of food, then removing it.

As the hour became late the activity in the corridor lessened to just the periodic checks. Gray went faster. He almost missed it. If he hadn't been watching the clock closely it would have passed him by. The time jumped. Gray paused, then rewound.

It occurred at 02:12. The corridor was empty, the light low. Then it was 02:18. Six minutes were missing. He went back and forth several times. There was a definite gap in the recording. Somebody had wiped it. Somebody who'd been to see Parker at an unholy hour and put the squeeze on him. Somebody who was good with managing digital recordings.

"You all right, Sol?" asked Fowler.

Thirty-Two

Then

The train drew to a slow halt, brakes squealing as metal bit metal, putting Fowler's teeth on edge. The driver released a gout of air from the hydraulic brakes, like the expelled breath of an out-of-shape runner. A repetitive bleeping sounded from inside the carriages before the double doors popped and slid apart. The train emptied. This was the end of the tracks for the London route, or the start if you were heading into the capital.

Fowler left the relative shelter of the entrance hall. Constructed in Victorian times, it was parquet floor beneath a tall, curved roof and a grand clock to let commuters know quite how delayed the service was. Heavy wooden doors shuttered behind him.

The kid was obvious the moment his feet hit the chewing-gum-spattered concrete platform. Rucksack thrown over one shoulder, pipe-cleaner-thin legs, and hunched in a too-thin jacket against the cold wind which blew along the track, funnelled by the building design which was really only intended to keep the rain off waiting passengers. His name was Nick Buckingham and he was Strang's debut mule, riding shotgun with Fowler for company. After a moment's orientation, Buckingham pulled up his hood, drew the strings tight, thrust his hands into coat pockets and followed the meagre flow towards the exit. Sheep, all heading in the same direction, and Fowler the wolf.

As Buckingham passed by, Fowler grabbed him by the arm. Buckingham glared at Fowler with bloodshot eyes. "What?" he said.

"I'm here to take you where you need to go," said Fowler. He didn't like this, being out in the open, managing a runner for Strang. It was dangerous.

Buckingham shook off Fowler's restraint. "I ain't doing shit for you, bro." Fowler rolled his eyes. Black street language from a white kid, trying to look tougher than he was. At least Buckingham wasn't rapping with it. The mood Fowler was in he'd have probably punched him.

"I'm here on behalf of Strang."

The kid's eyes widened, immediately dropping the attitude. "You should have said."

Fowler couldn't be bothered pointing out the obvious. He turned and walked back into the station hallway. He heard hurried footsteps behind him.

"Where's your car?" asked Buckingham as they got outside.

"No need. We're only going there."

Buckingham's sight followed Fowler's outstretched arm, pointing to the high-rise flats of Arlington House, looming large over Margate. Beyond were the lights of Dreamland, the amusement arcade which from a distance was more than it seemed; a disappointment close up. Fowler got going again, pausing briefly for a break in the traffic before crossing the road. Buckingham, a few paces behind, couldn't get over at the same time and he hopped from foot to foot while he paused. Fowler didn't wait.

A few yards around the corner was the front entrance. Fowler shoved hard against doors which stuck and squealed in protest. He crossed the lobby, paused by the lift until Buckingham entered, struggling with the door. Fowler pressed the up button. Above, the mechanism cranked into life. Eventually the lift doors opened, stopping halfway. Fowler turned sideways and slid through, sucking his belly in to do so. Buckingham was so skinny he'd no need to copy Fowler. Fowler thumbed the worn button for floor five. The doors closed and the lift jerked into motion.

The flat was just around the corner from the lift. Fowler took out a bunch of keys, unlocked two five-lever mortices and then a Yale. He allowed Buckingham to go first before closing up. He didn't bother to shoot the bolts top and bottom. He wouldn't be staying long enough. He'd tell Buckingham to, though.

Buckingham walked along the narrow corridor which cut through the flat. Two bedrooms, bathroom, kitchen, then living room with a scattering of cheap furniture and a view over the North Sea through large French windows. Beyond the brightly lit street below it was darkness.

"Have you got the stuff?" asked Fowler. Buckingham shrugged off the backpack and held it out. Fowler pushed out his hands. "I don't want it." Buckingham hefted a shoulder, dropped the pack to the floor. "If you want to eat go back downstairs and turn right. There's a chippy open all hours, and then a shopping centre."

"I haven't got any money."

"They didn't give you some?"

Buckingham looked away. "No."

Fowler knew it was a lie. Buckingham had spent it, probably on something powdery that went up his nose. Fowler took a twenty from his wallet and handed it over. He'd never get that back.

"How do I contact you?" asked Buckingham.

"You can't. Somebody will be in touch tomorrow."

"Okay."

"I'm off now. This is for the front door."

Buckingham took the key Fowler offered. Buckingham seemed small and lost in the expanse of the living room, bag at his feet. Fowler forced himself not to feel sympathy. He couldn't, he was just a facilitator, helping merchandise along the way. No more, no less.

Fowler pulled the door closed behind him, hoping he wouldn't see Buckingham again.

Thirty-Three

Now

"Sir?" Gray twisted in his chair. PC Boughton, the beat cop, was standing a few feet from Gray's desk.

"What can I do for you, Damian?" asked Gray.

"I may have something." Boughton held out a USB stick. "CCTV."

Gray plugged the stick into his laptop, clicked on the file. "Where did you get it?"

"There's a takeaway round the corner on Pump Lane, does Thai," said Boughton. "The Lotus."

"I know it." The food was good.

"After some trouble last year, they installed a camera."

"But we checked everywhere; Worthington assured me it was done."

"Mr Lao who runs the place did say we'd been in and spoken to his sons, but they'd assumed the camera was still broken. However, it had been fixed already. When I was walking past earlier, Mr Lao came out and gave me this. He knows I've been asking around."

The footage ran. It showed a person walking quickly past the camera, their back to the lens. Gray pressed pause. He caught Worthington's eye. "Jerry, come over here."

Worthington walked to Gray's desk. "What's up boss?" Fowler joined them too.

"Damian has pulled some footage from the Lotus takeaway."

Worthington frowned. "I went in there myself. I was told there was none."

"There is now. Take a look, tell me what you see."

Worthington bent over and watched the brief scene play out. When it was done he said, "He's talking on a mobile."

"That's what I thought." The person passing by had one hand up to their head. It was impossible to see the phone because of the pulled-up hood, but what else could it be? The hand was raised for too long. A mobile meant they could triangulate the call and obtain a number. Worthington checked the time stamp and wrote it down, then returned to his desk

"Thanks, Damian, I appreciate it," said Gray and shook Boughton's hand.

"Do you think it might be important?" asked Boughton.

"Yes, very possibly."

"Good." Boughton grinned. "It's been doing my head in, knowing there's a murderer on my patch." Boughton left the office.

Mobile operators were required to keep a record of every call and text for a year. The police had a direct link to the database via a single piece of software supplied by Charter Systems and didn't require a warrant to do so under RIPA – the Regulation of Investigatory Powers Act. The process was automated but operated under apparently strict guidelines.

However, all that was required was for one officer, Gray in this case, to give permission to another to gain access by filling in the required paperwork. Gray pulled the form up, entered the relevant data and fired it off. He raised a thumb at Worthington, who tapped away on his computer.

By the time Gray reached Worthington's desk, the DC was already into the system and had a list of numbers onscreen. "Nearest masts are Herbert Place, Addington Square and All Saints Avenue," said Worthington. The first two just a few streets away from Union Row and the latter at the foot of Arlington House. Three masts were enough to triangulate the position of a phone. "What time was it again?"

"10.44 on Pump Lane," said Gray.

Worthington ran his finger down the list. "This will be the one." Gray wrote the number down. "It's a burner." So no identified ownership; a pay-as-you-go SIM.

Worthington tapped the number into the database. "It hasn't been used since the date of Oakley's murder."

"What about the IMEI?"

The International Mobile Equipment Identity was a unique number associated with the phone itself. The user could easily change the SIM card but the IMEI stayed with the phone for its lifetime. Worthington obtained the details and checked it against the National Mobile Property Register. "This is interesting."

Gray got in closer. The owner was Jason Harwood. He'd reported it stolen a month ago.

"Perhaps it never was nicked," said Worthington.

"But Harwood didn't murder Oakley; he has a cast-iron alibi."

"I don't know what this means, sir."

"Me neither." Gray straightened up. "But let's bring Harwood in, see what the hell is going on."

Gray's landline rang. He went back to his desk, picked it up. "Sol," said DS Morgan at the front desk. "There's someone here asking for you. A Jason Harwood. Do you know him?"

Thirty-Four

Now When Gray and Worthington entered the interview room, Harwood stopped pacing and looked them over. He was wearing the same tracksuit combination as the previous time Gray had seen him, unless Harwood was like Mark Zuckerberg and Steve Jobs, simply owning a multiple of the same clothing for straightforward decision making. Somehow Gray doubted it.

"I want to talk alone," said Harwood. He pointed at Gray. "Just with you."

"Sir?" said Worthington.

"Wait outside please, Jerry," said Gray. Worthington withdrew, closing the door behind him. Harwood resumed his pacing again. "Why don't you sit down?"

Harwood ignored Gray's suggestion but paused to chew a cuticle. "Where's Jackie?"

"In a cell. She's been arrested for attempted assault. According to her record it's not the first time she's been locked up for threatening behaviour."

"She has a temper on her," admitted Harwood. "The Social have my kids?"

"Nobody knew where you were."

"I was having a few beers." Harwood ran his fingers through his hair. "It's all going to shit." He flopped down into a chair.

"Parker's been stabbed."

"I know."

"So what's this about, Mr Harwood?"

"You aren't taping me, right?"

"Not at the moment."

"What about the CCTV?" Harwood nodded at the camera in the angle where ceiling met wall.

"It isn't turned on."

"Good, 'cos I ain't going on record. If you want to tape what I say, I'm out."

"I can live with that."

"Okay." Harwood nodded, more to himself than Gray. "Somebody got to Parker."

"Clearly."

"No, I mean he was shut up. He knew things."

"Like what?"

"Oakley. The kid who got stabbed." He paused. "Parker knew who did it."

"Do you?"

"No. He wouldn't say and I didn't want him to tell me. He called me the night before he was knifed. He was in a right state."

"What did he say?"

"Just what I told you, that he was shitting himself about getting shanked. He'd been warned."

"By who?"

BURY THE BODIES 217

"Dunno." Harwood shrugged. "Like I said, the less information I had the better. Safer."

Gray decided there wasn't any more to get from Harwood about Parker. "A few months ago you reported a phone stolen."

Harwood frowned. "Can't remember."

"I've got a report that says you did." Gray read out the phone number.

"Yeah, that's mine; I thought I'd lost it. There was no credit on the SIM anyway."

"And you haven't seen it since?"

"I told you, no."

"Why did you report it stolen?"

"Claim on the insurance, of course."

"We believe the phone was used immediately after Oakley's murder."

"I've got an alibi. You can't fix that on me."

"Nobody's attempting to do so, but anything you can remember might be a help."

Harwood thought for a few moments but eventually shook his head. "No, man, nothing's coming back."

Gray sat down opposite Harwood and considered his next step. "Ray Ingham, he's a friend of yours, right?"

Harwood pulled a face. "He's a tosser."

"You grew up together. You hang out with the same people."

"We were friends, then he turned on me."

"How?"

Harwood shook his head, looked down at his feet. "He was shagging Jackie. They're over now, but it's hard to forget, you know?"

"When we were searching your flat you said the baby wasn't yours. Is she..."

Harwood brought his eyes up to Gray's. It seemed like he was about to cry. "Ingham's? Yeah. And he doesn't know. That's the one decent thing Jackie didn't do, telling everybody on the estate."

There was a brief knock at the door before it opened sharply. Gray was about to shout at Worthington for the interruption but it was Fowler. He glanced past Gray to Harwood before he said, "Can I have a word when you're done, sir?"

"We'll be another few minutes yet."

"That works. Sorry to intrude." Fowler withdrew.

Gray returned his attention to Harwood. He'd shrunk back into his seat, his face the colour of cheap white paint.

"I'm off," said Harwood. He leapt up, made to pass Gray who stood also.

Gray put a hand out, grabbed Harwood's forearm. "What's the matter?"

"Nothing, I just want to get my kids." But he was lying. He was shaking with fear.

"We're not done yet. Who do you think took your phone?" Harwood didn't answer. "Was it Ingham?"

"No way, I wouldn't have him inside the flat for the last year."

Gray considered this. As the mobile went missing a matter of weeks ago it couldn't have been Ingham. "Unless Jackie was letting him in behind your back?"

"Believe me, I'd have known. I've eyes on them both. We're done here."

Gray released Harwood. There was nothing he could do to stop Harwood leaving. "Thanks for your help." He opened the door. Worthington was outside. "Can you take Mr Parker to the front desk. He needs to get in touch with Social."

"No problem," said Worthington.

Then Gray went looking for Fowler. He didn't have to go far because a few yards along through a set of glass double doors Fowler was leaning against the corridor wall beside the entrance to the gent's bathroom. He was clearly waiting for Gray.

"What do you want, Mike?" asked Gray.

Fowler didn't answer, entering the bathroom instead. Gray followed, wondering what the hell was going on. Leaning over a sink, Fowler had his back turned to Gray. He started a tap, pushed soap from a dispenser into his palm. Gray watched him in the smoky mirror fixed to the wall above the sink.

"*Mike*," repeated Gray.

"Parker's dead. He passed away a half hour ago."

"Christ." Gray would have to call the prison governor, have a talk with her. "But that could have waited. Did you have to interrupt my conversation with Harwood?"

"It was necessary."

"Why?"

"Because you need to leave this, Sol," said Fowler over the sound of flowing water. He rubbed his hands together under the stream.

"I don't understand."

Fowler glanced up into the mirror above the sink, met Gray's eyes. He turned off the tap, shook excess water from his hands before shifting to the hand towel dispenser, pulling a couple out and slowly drying his hands. He dropped them into the waste bin before turning his full attention to Gray.

Without warning, Fowler leapt forward, catching Gray off guard. Gray's back hit the wall with a thud, Fowler's forearm up under his chin, pressing into his neck.

"Don't start digging into the Parker case, Sol," snarled Fowler. "He's just a druggie. If you keep on going you're not going to like what you find."

"Fuck off, Mike."

"I thought you'd say that." Fowler released Gray. "I'll see you later." Fowler left, leaving Gray standing in the bathroom.

Thirty-Five

Now
Gray picked up his ruined suit from where he'd left it yesterday, on the bedroom floor in his flat. He felt around in the jacket pockets until he touched the shotgun cartridge. He withdrew the plastic and metal cylinder, dropped the jacket again. He'd held ammunition like this many times before. He used to shoot clay pigeons with Carslake for fun. The cartridge was a symbol, which was why McGavin had left it with him.

In his living room, Gray crossed to the drinks cabinet and poured himself a large whisky; didn't bother to add water. He wasn't drinking for pleasure. He sat down on the sofa, placed the cartridge in the centre of the coffee table by a chess set. The pieces were spread around the board, a game in progress. Gray was recreating a game between grand masters Garry Kasparov and Anatoly Karpov.

Gray called Pennance on his mobile. "Can I speak to Hope, Marcus?"

"Just a second," said Pennance.

His daughter came on the line. "Hello, Dad. Are you okay?"

"I'm fine, thanks. How about you?"

"Can I come home yet?"

Home, Gray was surprised to hear Hope use the word. She can't have thought about Broadstairs like that for years. And she'd ignored his question.

"Hopefully soon."

"What's going on?"

"I haven't got long, Hope. There's something I need to tell you."

"Now?"

"Yes."

"Why?"

Gray didn't want to say *just in case*. "It's about Tom." He heard her intake of breath down the line. "A man called Lewis Strang may hold the answer to finding him."

"Strang, who's he? And how does he know Tom?"

"Marcus can tell you all about him, I don't have all the answers yet."

"Why are you saying this now? You're scaring me."

"I don't mean to, and you've got Marcus."

"Dad."

"I have to go. Can you put him back on?"

"Okay." Hope handed the phone over before Gray could reply.

"Sol," said Pennance. "What's up?"

Gray picked up the shotgun cartridge, twisted it in his fingers. "I think I'm getting to the bottom of the barrel here."

"Are you going to scrape it?"

"I have to. Look after her for me."

"Of course."

Gray disconnected but immediately tapped in another number. It was answered quickly.

BURY THE BODIES

"Hamish Gellatly." A Scottish burr.

"Hi, Hamish, we don't know each other. My name's Solomon Gray, Hope's father."

"Oh," surprise in Hamish's voice. "Hello Mr Gray. How can I help you?"

"Sol is fine. And it's more the other way around, hopefully."

"O-kay." By Hamish's tone he was clearly wondering what was going on.

"Do you love my daughter?"

"That's a rather direct and abrupt question, if I may say so."

"I don't have time to mess around."

Hamish sighed. "It's rather complicated."

"Actually Hamish, a simple yes or no will do."

"Look, Mr Gray I don't know what this is about but…"

"Do you love her, or not?"

Hamish was silent for a few moments before he finally said, "Yes, I do."

"I'm glad to hear it. You're going to come down here and take her back home."

"She doesn't want me to."

"Rubbish, Hamish. She's in pieces right now. Get your backside to Broadstairs and talk to her."

"I have patients."

"You have a partner too. And a child on the way."

"It'll take me a day to get sorted."

"Let me know when you're going to arrive."

"And you're sure she'll speak to me?"

"I'll make certain of it."

"Thank you, Mr Gray – sorry – Sol."

"Let me give you another number in case you can't reach me." Gray read out Pennance's details. "I'll see you soon."

If everything went tits up Pennance would take over. Either way, Hope should be fine. He headed out onto the balcony with his whisky. He looked down. Leaning against the metal railings on the cliff edge was Mike Fowler. He lifted a phone to his ear. Gray's mobile rang inside.

"Come on up," said Gray when he answered. "I've been expecting you."

FOWLER CLOSED THE FRONT door behind him. "Sol," said Fowler. Gray, sitting on the sofa, didn't reply. Fowler glanced around the living room. "Is Hope here?"

"I'm not stupid."

"Do you mind if I take a look?"

"Be my guest."

Fowler entered each room in the flat, one after the other, slowly pushing back every door with the heel of his palm, as if expecting somebody to leap out. When he returned, he paused by the coffee table. He stared at the cartridge, but didn't pick it up.

"Why, Mike?"

"The same as you, Sol."

"Our situations aren't comparable."

"I couldn't help but get drawn in." Fowler shook his head. "Carslake—"

Gray cut him off. "Merely opened the door. You chose to walk through."

BURY THE BODIES

"Don't you think I haven't regretted it a thousand times since?"

"I've no idea."

Fowler went to the drinks cabinet, poured himself a large shot. He sank half of the measure, wiped his mouth with the back of his hand. "This is it now, I'm getting out."

"After one last job?"

Fowler leaned against the cabinet. "You're a fool, Sol."

"For not keeping quiet?"

"For not taking McGavin's side. He'd have paid you, and well. A couple of years and you'd have had a nice pile."

"Like you?" Fowler didn't reply. Gray said, "I'm not interested in cash."

"Retire then!"

"I'd be bored stupid."

"Jesus, Sol, just something that wouldn't have led us to this, then."

"To what, Mike?"

Fowler shook his head. "I can't protect you anymore." He finished the whisky; put the glass down beside him.

"Is that what you've been trying to do?" Gray hoped his derision rang loud and clear.

"Of course." Fowler's shoulders hunched. "If you'd have let it go."

"I couldn't."

"I told McGavin that. I can read you like a book, Sol." Fowler pushed himself off the cabinet, straightened himself up. He pulled out a mobile, tapped in a number. It was answered quickly. Fowler said, "I have him." He held out the phone for Gray. He took it.

"Solomon?" It was McGavin.

"What do you want?"

"For you to meet me."

"What if I don't?"

"Then I can't guarantee Hope's safety."

"I'm not worried about her."

"You should be. She can't hide forever." McGavin paused a heartbeat. "It's you or her."

Gray had a choice, but didn't. "Where?"

"The place the lad Buckingham took a dive."

McGavin disconnected. Gray handed the mobile back to Fowler, picked up his glass.

"I'll see you there," said Fowler. Gray swirled his whisky, staring into its depths. Fowler left. Gray eventually downed the measure and went to get his car keys before following his ex-friend out of the door.

Thirty-Six

Now

There was a space in a bay on All Saints' Avenue at the foot of Arlington House which Gray pulled into. He switched off the engine, got out and pocketed the keys. Gray couldn't see Fowler. The car park entrance was still cordoned off.

When Gray entered the lobby, Fowler was awaiting him. Neither spoke, as if they were strangers. Gray called the lift by pressing the up arrow. The mechanism kicked in high above them, the rattle of the gears and chains like Marley's ghost. When the lift reached them the doors jerked open, then stuck halfway. Gray squeezed through the gap, waited for Fowler. The interior smelt of marijuana. Graffiti had been scratched onto the walls: a phone number offering sexual favours (presumably for a fee), a statement that somebody called Andrew was gay and MUFC – Gray assumed for Manchester United, not Margate or Macclesfield.

Gray pressed a thumb into the worn button for the fifth floor, the number barely legible. The doors closed before the metal box lurched upwards. The lift shuddered to a halt a half minute later, and the doors parted once more. Fowler was first out, leading the way. Fowler took him to the flat where Nick Buckingham had been thrown off the balcony a year ago.

Fowler knocked once, a short, sharp rap. Ingham opened up, eyeballing Gray over Fowler's shoulder.

Once inside, Ingham pushed the door to, the Yale lock clicking into place before Ingham shot bolts top and bottom. He winked at Gray. Braced by Fowler and Ingham, Gray was taken along the corridor, past bedrooms, bathroom and kitchen and into the living room at the far end. It wasn't much different to the last time he'd been here. A large, glass window stared out over a narrow balcony, the busy road and the North Sea beneath. Sticks of furniture placed around the room – designs from the 1970s made in bulk – low cost and beige. A sofa, couple of chairs, a coffee table in stainless steel and smoked glass. The mould patches where wall met ceiling remained.

McGavin was waiting for him by the window. "They say location is everything, Sol. Although in this case, other than the view, Arlington House is the exception to the rule."

"You didn't bring me here for property advice, McGavin."

McGavin laughed. "To the point, as always. And you're right, of course. This is about burying the past, Solomon." McGavin pulled open the large French window. It squeaked on poorly lubricated runners. Immediately wind whistled into the room. McGavin stepped outside onto the narrow balcony. "Come over here, would you?" Ingham needlessly shoved Gray again.

Gray swung around and said, "Do that again and I'll break your arm."

"All right, Grandad," said Ingham. "Calm down."

Gray joined McGavin, but stayed just within the flat. He wasn't keen on heights at the best of times. The balcony was a rickety affair, a lump of concrete shoved onto the outside of a cheap building constructed decades ago in an era when throwing up places to live in double-quick time was key. There was a metal railing around the edge which was spotted with rust and cracks across the base.

"Why are we here?" asked Gray.

McGavin attempted surprise. "For you of course, Solomon." McGavin rattled the balcony railings, metal ground against concrete. "Doesn't sound safe, does it?" He turned back to Gray. "What I always do is bury the bodies and bury them deep, so they're never found."

"Very poetic."

"Quite, and you're the last."

"What is this? Tell a story day?"

"I was thinking suicide, a man so depressed he throws himself off the side of a building at the scene of a previous investigation."

"That's not really burying me, McGavin."

"It was a metaphor," sighed McGavin. "CCTV will show you driving over here on your own. You spend a bit of time in the flat, deciding your fate before ..." McGavin whistled, high pitch dropping to a lower tone, like Gray was falling, before he slapped his hands together. Splat. "What do you think?"

"For you it's quite subtle."

McGavin grinned. He stepped back inside, leaving the windows open. Gray was sure the balcony had shifted under McGavin's weight. The temperature in the room was dropping, the wind cold this high up. "Ah, there's more. Mike here can attest to your ongoing depression and gloominess as, I'm sure, could many of your colleagues. It would be a relatively straightforward task to manipulate an enquiry. But, then again, you know that already, don't you, Solomon?"

"Speaking of subtlety, Ingham's attempt to frame Jason Harwood for murder wasn't so effective," said Gray. "Dropping his glove at the scene threw me off briefly, but not for long." Gray turned to Ingham. "Looking forward to prison?"

"What are you on about?" asked Ingham. To Gray he seemed genuinely puzzled. "I didn't kill the black kid. You're talking shite."

Then there was only one other person who'd had access to both Harwood's old phone and his gloves.

"I've had enough of this." McGavin retreated towards the far end of the room, blocking the exit. "Get it done," he said. Fowler stayed where he was, between McGavin and Gray, seemingly not keen to get involved.

"Why don't you just go over by yourself?" asked Ingham. "Make it easier for us all."

"I never go down without a fight."

"I hoped you'd say that." Ingham came for Gray, slowly.

"What's your daughter's name, by the way?" asked Gray. Ingham didn't reply, focused on his task. "The one Jackie Lycett had after your affair?" Ingham paused, his arms dropped as the revelation passed through his mind. Gray feigned surprise. "Oh, she never told you? She's been arrested so Harwood is looking after your child like he has since she was born, but you're good with that, right?"

While Ingham hesitated, Gray took his chance and ran at him, dropping a shoulder. He struck Ingham in the chest. The two of them went down. But Ingham was fast and he was angry. Gray's earlier words had stung and they seemed to lend Ingham extra strength. He was like a boxer – a quick count and up and on his toes, appearing unaffected. Ingham took up the pugilist's stance, fists up, elbows in.

"Come on," said Ingham, beckoning Gray.

Gray slowly rose. Before he could get his defence up, Ingham lashed out, his right fist a blur. Gray barely saw the swing, only able to move an inch or so before the blow caught him on the cheekbone. The pain was immediate and Ingham followed up with another, rattling Gray's teeth. His world lurched. Gray was dazed, ears ringing. Ingham smacked Gray again, right in the solar plexus. Gray lost the air from his lungs, like somebody had reached inside and blocked his throat. He couldn't breathe, unable to replace the expended oxygen. He sank to his knees, gasping.

While Gray fought for breath, Ingham marched over, grabbed him by the shoulder and dragged him towards the open window. Gray could hardly resist as his body was still fighting for equilibrium. When they reached the balcony, Gray desperately threw out a hand, grabbed onto the door surround, impeding Ingham for a moment. But Ingham cracked Gray's knuckles and he let go.

The balcony creaked and groaned as Ingham jerked Gray out into the wind. Ingham reached down and got Gray by the belt of his trousers. He began to heave. Gray hung on tight to the balcony railing, wrapping his arms around the rusty metal which bit into his skin. He ignored the pain as the shards sliced skin. The balcony buckled under the onslaught.

"Give me a hand!" shouted Ingham.

Fowler slowly moved forward. His intervention would tip the balance. Gray almost let go then. He couldn't fend off the two of them. Fowler paused as he reached the window.

"Get his other leg," said Ingham. "Then we'll have him over."

"Mike!" said Gray.

"I'm sorry," replied Fowler. Then he shoved Ingham in the back. Ingham, not expecting Fowler's move, lost his grip on Gray and went half over the railing. Gray crawled away, getting off the balcony, as Fowler did exactly what Ingham has requested, got hold of a leg – but it was Ingham's. Fowler heaved upwards, throwing Ingham into empty space. Ingham screamed all the way down until his wail was sharply cut off. Moments later there was the sound of a car horn and screaming.

Gray lay on the floor, panting. McGavin was gone; Gray had no idea when he'd left. Gray sat up, turned to face the outside. Fowler was standing on the balcony, staring down after Ingham, his back to Gray. Then a loud crack and the balcony lurched again, Fowler taking on a drunken angle. The balcony was coming away, the couplings shearing under Fowler's weight. He grabbed hold of the railing before glancing over his shoulder, his face twisted in fear.

"Sol!" shouted Fowler. With a screech and another bang the balcony parted from the wall and plummeted. Gray threw himself forward, arm outstretched, in a vain attempt to grab Fowler. But it was too late. Gravity had hold and it wasn't letting go.

Gray watched Fowler soundlessly fall to the ground below. The balcony smashed onto the pavement, landing on top of Ingham's prostrate form, spreading debris across the road, Fowler landing a moment later. His body hit the railings before spinning away. From the shape of Fowler's sprawled form, his limbs at odd angles and his neck resting on his shoulder, it was obvious he was dead.

A passing car slewed to a halt, blocked by a couple who'd already stopped because of Ingham. The driver leapt out, staring at the mess, then the gap where the balcony had once been. He pulled a phone out from his pocket and put it to his ear.

Gray inched inside and rolled onto his back. He stared at the ceiling until the sirens arrived.

Thirty-Seven

Hours later, Gray was sitting with Hamson in one of the interview rooms, door closed, recorder off as Gray had requested. Hamson had listened to Gray recount the events leading up to Ingham and Fowler's deaths open-mouthed. She hadn't asked a single question.

"I don't know about you," said Hamson, "but I need a drink. It's hard to believe. All those years of lies."

"He fooled everyone, Von."

Hamson put her head in her hands. "Marsh is going to be looking for scapegoats over this. A dirty cop under my watch."

"We're not going to work that way." Hamson looked up at Gray. "Mike saved my life, losing his own, which is how we're telling it."

"I can't do that, Sol."

"Von, he died a hero. Nobody needs to know about his other side. What purpose does it serve now?"

"What about McGavin?"

"Who'd listen to him?" McGavin was on the run, an APB out for his arrest but so far not a trace found at his house or businesses. "Mike was my backup; he saved me from Ingham but died in the process. That's what I'm saying, Von." Hamson stared at Gray for a few moments. "It's the right thing to do."

Eventually Hamson said, "Okay."

"Thank you." Gray rose. "Before we start officially, I know who killed Oakley. I need you with me."

Jackie Lycett was waiting in the room next door. Gray and Hamson took chairs opposite. An Indian female duty lawyer wearing a sober black jacket and white shirt combination sat beside Lycett. She introduced herself as Miss Sharma.

"I've been sitting here ages," spat Lycett. "What the fuck's going on? Where's my kids?" she asked.

"They're with Mr Harwood," said Gray. He started the machine recording. "Miss Lycett, who's the father of your youngest child?"

"What's that got to do with anything?"

"Answer the question, please."

"Jason is."

"That's not true."

Lycett got to her feet. "You're calling me a liar?" she shouted.

"Sit down."

Lycett stayed on her feet until Sharma said, "Miss Lycett, I can't represent you if you don't answer the officer's questions." Lycett sat.

"And yes, I am calling you a liar. I have it on very good authority that the father of your child is actually Ray Ingham." Lycett's face coloured, but she said nothing. Gray continued, "I also know you and Mr Harwood were having relationship issues, directly as a result of your affair." Lycett dug her fingernails into her palms. "Do you recognise these?" Gray placed two evidence bags before her. One containing Harwood's glove, the other the "stolen" mobile.

"No." Lycett crossed her arms, turned away.

"I think you do. I believe you murdered LaShaun Oakley and left the glove at the scene, then used Mr Harwood's phone to directly implicate him so you could be with Mr Ingham."

"No."

"The trouble was you weren't aware that Mr Harwood was actually at the pub when you were stabbing the victim. You two barely spoke with each other as it was, and Mr Harwood had a frenetic social life, so why would you? And I'd bet you also didn't know Mr Harwood had reported the phone stolen. He could barely remember himself."

"I've no idea what you're on about." Lycett turned to her lawyer. "Tell him, I didn't do nothing."

"Have you any evidence to back up your claims?" asked Sharma.

"I'm coming to that. Where were you around 10.30 on Wednesday last week, Miss Lycett?"

"I was at home, with the kids. Jason was out on the piss, as you said. Where else would I be?"

"In the last hour I sent one of my colleagues over to Staner Court to interview your neighbours. It transpires that Mrs Jessop, who lives opposite, babysat for you at the time when Oakley was attacked. So you weren't at home."

"She's full of shit," said Lycett.

"And we've got CCTV footage of Mr Oakley's assailant, which we've analysed to assess height and build. The measurements match yours. Finally, we're in the process of contacting the taxi firms to ask who they collected from your area and drove into Margate. Any time soon, I'm expecting to come up with the answer. Most of the vehicles have cameras these days. And, right now, crime scene investigators are searching your flat for anything else they might turn up." Gray turned to Hamson. "I think that's sufficient, don't you ma'am?"

"Agreed," said Hamson.

"Jackie Lycett, I am arresting you for the murder of LaShaun Oakley." Gray read Lycett her rights. She said nothing.

After Lycett had been led away Hamson said, "Well done, Sol."

"Before we carry on, can I make a call?"

"Sure," said Hamson. "I'll see you next door in a few minutes."

When Hamson had gone, Gray pulled out his mobile. "Marcus, it's Sol. Can you bring Hope back home?"

"Tomorrow okay?"

"Great, thanks."

"You sound tired, Sol. Like you need a break."

"Hopefully I'll get one soon. See you later."

Gray disconnected. He noticed a text had come in, from Hamish. He was on the way down to Thanet now and would be over in the morning. He asked Gray to tell him where and when to meet.

Then Gray went to see Hamson. To make up a story for the last time.

Thirty-Eight

Now

Gray rose late the following morning. Hamson had given him the day off. Wyatt had stayed over, but she wasn't in bed when he woke. He found her on the balcony, nursing a cup of tea. Hope was with her. Gray forced himself to go outside, the memory of his fight with Fowler still sharp in his memory. Wyatt stood, hugged Gray.

"Are you okay, Dad?"

"I'm fine thanks. Where's Marcus?"

"He's gone. We didn't want to disturb you."

"I'll make you a coffee," said Wyatt, rising. She kissed Gray on the cheek as she passed. "We've been talking about you, of course."

"I'd have expected nothing less."

Wyatt's chair was positioned right in the sun which was poking through the clouds.

"Why don't we go for a walk later?" asked Gray.

"I'd like that. What about Stone Bay? We used to go there all the time as kids."

And that was where Tanya, briefly Gray's girlfriend, had been murdered. But Gray felt like he could finally move on from the past. "Okay," he said. "But a coffee and a shower first." *And a text to Hamish.*

LATER, WHEN WYATT HAD taken her leave, Gray and Hope walked through Broadstairs, past Morelli's, a family-run ice-cream parlour that had barely changed since the 60s, then the Albion Hotel with the best views in Broadstairs, the mini arcade of flashing lights and rattling slots, before turning down Harbour Street, a hill which led down to the jetty from which they stepped onto the sand.

Hope linked her arm through Gray's and they walked in silence for a while, enjoying the sound of the breaking waves.

When they reached Stone Bay they sat for a while on the sea wall watching people walk as close to the curling waves as possible without getting wet. A handful of Common Gulls perched in the sand, ignoring the passers-by.

Eventually Hope said, "I've made my decision, Dad. I'm keeping the baby." Gray squeezed her hand, not trusting himself to speak. "I'm a due for a scan next week. Will you come with me?"

"Of course. I've told you already. Whatever you need."

"Thanks, Dad."

"I'll always be here for you."

They sat like that for a while until a shadow fell across them.

"Hello, Hope."

Hope, shielding her eyes from the sun said, "Hamish! What are you doing here?"

"That would be down to me," admitted Gray.

"I just want to talk," said Hamish. "May I?" He pointed at the spot next to her.

"Free country. Do what you want," said Hope.

Hamish sat, his feet dangling. He was a tall man, a good few inches over six feet, broad shoulders, a strong jaw, high forehead and dark hair shot through with some white.

"I'll leave you two alone," said Gray.

"You don't need to," said Hope.

"No, you have a lot to talk about. I'll see you back at the flat."

Gray pushed himself up, brushed the sand from his palms and got walking. When he glanced over his shoulder he saw Hope leaning into Hamish, his arm around her. It seemed like everything was going to be all right.

Thirty-Nine

"Black suits you, Sol," said Wyatt as she reached out and straightened Gray's tie.

He was wearing his dress uniform, an item that hadn't been out of storage for years. It'd needed dry cleaning. But amazingly, the moths hadn't been at it.

A gust of wind whipped along Vicarage Street where Gray and his fellow mourners were assembled in a disordered group, mostly police, spread from the pavement into the grounds of St Peter's Church, a flint-encased building whose origins stretched back a thousand years. A few stood outside the pub directly across the road, drinks in hand.

"Looks like rain," Gray said. The sky was overcast; the clouds tinged the colour of ash. The hearse was late. He was to be a pall bearer.

"What do you think Fowler's lawyer is going to tell you?" asked Wyatt.

A couple of days after Fowler's demise, a man named Keogh had called Gray out of the blue. Keogh had said he was Fowler's representative and Gray was listed in his last will and testament.

"I've no idea, but I'll find out soon enough."

"How's Hope?"

"She's fine, happy." Hope had gone back to Edinburgh with Hamish. Gray missed her greatly.

"Look out," said Wyatt, glancing past him. "Trouble's on the way."

"Trouble" turned out to be Superintendent Marsh.

"Morning, sir," said Gray.

"On a day like this, Sol, no titles please."

"Fine by me."

"Have you got a moment? I won't keep you long."

"Sure," said Gray.

Marsh turned, headed past the church, towards the graveyard, along a narrow, tarmac path. He paused beyond the furthest outreach of grievers, outside a small, walled-off section for the cremations.

"We can keep an eye on the gate from here," said Marsh. "In case the hearse turns up." Marsh was a pall bearer too.

"Yes, sir. Sorry... Bernard."

"It's me who should be apologising to you. I made a mistake, a rather large one." Gray blinked. The Superintendent wasn't one for admitting to human frailty. "I was wrong about you." Gray opened his mouth to protest. Marsh raised a hand to stop him. "Tackling Ingham and McGavin was brave, and you brought in Oakley's killer. Yvonne was right to put you forward for promotion. You pair are my best men." Gray held back from pointing out Hamson was a woman. Marsh was on a roll. "Thanet CID is going to need rebuilding from the ground up and I'd like the two of you to lead that effort. As a result I'm making your inspector's position permanent, which I should have done in the first place. What do you say?"

"I don't know, sir."

It was Marsh's turn to be taken aback. "I thought you'd be delighted."

"Don't get me wrong, I appreciate your confidence in me, but I've never done the job for promotion. And given recent events I'm not sure what I want to do with myself."

Marsh nodded. "I understand, Sol." The Superintendent held out his hand. "Well, whatever you choose, you have my best wishes." The pair shook.

"Sorry to interrupt." It was Wyatt a few feet away. "The hearse is here."

GRAY, MARSH AND FOUR other officers had borne Fowler's coffin inside. The vicar had read his service standing in the pulpit below the stained-glass windows depicting 2000-year-old events and a few hymns had been sung beneath a soaring roof. Gray was aware that proceedings weren't really a reflection of Fowler. But, had he truly known him?

The answer, of course, was no. He and Hamson had discussed the enigma of Fowler endlessly over recent days. What they'd missed, how they had done so. Wondering at how Fowler had managed to keep his secrets so well. Gray was due to read a eulogy. He'd agonised over what to say. Still was.

The vicar, a middle-aged man with a deep cleft in his chin, beckoned Gray to his feet when it was time. Hamson, seated beside Gray, smiled. Wyatt, sitting on his other side, squeezed his hand.

Gray stood, passed Marsh and Yarrow and climbed the pulpit steps. He withdrew a piece of paper from his inside pocket, placed it on the lectern and smoothed out the creases. All eyes were on Gray, a sea of pale, expectant faces riding waves of black cloth. The nave was packed, cops even stood at the rear. Fowler had been an irascible but popular colleague. The vicar, standing to one side, nodded at Gray, as if he needed encouragement to speak. Gray placed both hands on the lectern, leaned forward and kept his vision on the mix of lies and truth on the paper in front of him.

Somebody coughed. Gray glanced up again. Wyatt raised a covert thumb at him. But Gray was sick of the subterfuge, his own and others. Hadn't he joined the police to seek out the truth? Feet shifted within the congregation, the silence stretching.

Hamson gave Gray a minute shake of the head; the frown on her face was unmistakable, however.

Not now, not here.

Not ever...

They'd talked about this too. Hamson had been forthright. For all their sakes Fowler had to be literally buried. They needed to move on. They had to make things better, just as Marsh had suggested earlier.

And Gray knew she was correct. In the end, despite everything, Fowler had saved Gray and he would be forever grateful for that. He smoothed out the paper once more before he began to speak.

With each word Gray's voice grew stronger and Mike Fowler, just for a few minutes, came alive again.

Forty

Now
The offices of Keogh and Lane were located on the narrow and busy road called Moat Sole, just behind the council buildings in the quaint ancient walled town of Sandwich. The building itself was what had been a terraced house, residences either side. Except for the company name inscribed in gold lettering on the downstairs windows, Keogh and Lane was indistinguishable from its neighbours.

Gray was led into Keogh's book-lined office on the first floor right on time. Slatted blinds across the window cut out some of the morning light. The traffic noise was muted by double glazing.

Keogh, a spindly man who appeared to be in his fifties, placed half-moon glasses on the desk before he stood and came out into the room to welcome Gray. He had a limp and moved slowly. "Old war wound," joked Keogh as he took Gray's hand in both of his and shook. "Thank you for coming, Mr Gray. Please, sit down."

The solicitor waved at a chair in front of his desk and reclaimed his seat, lowering himself down with a slight grimace. Gray settled into the wooden chair. Keogh already had a file open on his desk, which was empty of all other paperwork.

"Is anybody else coming?" asked Gray, expecting Fowler's ex-wife at least to be present.

"Just you, Mr Gray. The will was read yesterday."

"I thought that's what I was here for."

"Not entirely. I am supposed to hand you this." Keogh held out an envelope, the standard letter size. Gray took it from Keogh's unresisting fingers.

Keogh stood and said, "I'll leave you alone for a few minutes, so you may read in peace." He limped to the door, closing it behind him.

Gray turned the envelope over in his hands. It was white and plain. Gray's name on the front. Gray recognised Fowler's neat script. There was nothing on the back. Gray slid a finger under the seal. Inside was a single piece of paper.

It was an adoption certificate, dated eleven years ago.

GRAY HAD LEFT HIS CAR in the car park adjacent to what was loosely termed the harbour, really just a wharf on a narrow tidal mud river. Years ago, Sandwich had been on the coast and an important port. Not anymore.

He read the certificate again. His son was still called Tom, but his surname had changed. The parents were listed – Donna and Lewis Massey – but not a precise address. The adoption had occurred in the county of Derbyshire, half way up England, much of it located on a spine of hills called the Peak District. Massey wasn't a tremendously common name; it should give Gray something to work on.

His phone rang. It was Pennance.

"Marcus," said Gray.

"I wanted to let you know that we arrested Strang earlier today."

BURY THE BODIES

"That's good news, well done."

"You all right, Sol?"

"Yes, sorry, just distracted."

"I thought you'd be chomping at the bit to speak with him."

"I'm not sure I need to anymore. I've got hold of an adoption certificate which I'm pretty certain means I can find Tom."

"That's bloody amazing!"

"To be honest I'm trying hard not to celebrate too much, Marcus. I've hit so many dead ends in the past."

"Where did you get the paperwork from?"

"Fowler left it for me."

"Then this is it, Sol. This is the end of the road."

Forty-One

Now Pennance wasn't quite right. Gray had to travel the road a little further before he reached his destination. There had been a few more people called Massey in Derbyshire than he'd thought. Apparently the family had come over in 1066 with William the Conqueror; there was even a major house in nearby Cheshire they'd once owned, before the line had died out.

The taxi dropped Gray off on a quiet, residential street. Gray shrugged the backpack over his shoulder and checked the address. This was it. The spa town of Buxton. He'd booked a nearby hotel for an overnight stay.

The rain was a persistent drizzle that had stippled the taxi's windscreen all the way from the train station to here. The driver had moaned about the weather. It rained a lot in Buxton, up in the Derbyshire Peak District. According to the driver it was the highest market town in England and, in his words, copped the lot when it came to bad weather.

After the car had driven away, Gray stood staring at the house, a suburban semi-detached with a faux well in the front garden. All these years and he was about to knock on a door and meet his son.

Gray pushed at the metal gate which separated pavement from property. The hinges squeaked. Gray followed the short path. He paused again before he rapped his knuckles on the door. Nobody answered, so he knocked again.

He heard urgent footsteps before the door opened and a middle-aged woman peeked around, a blue towel wrapped around her head. "Sorry, I was just getting out of the shower." The towel slipped and she put a hand up to straighten it. Gray recognised her as Donna Massey.

"I was looking for Tom," said Gray.

"Sorry, you've just missed him. He headed out ten minutes ago with his girlfriend, Monica."

"Oh, when will he be back?" Gray felt deflated.

"I've no idea. Sometimes he stays at hers." She grinned. "Teenagers, law unto themselves."

"So I understand."

"I know where they're going, though," she said. "If that would help?"

"TABLE FOR ONE?" ASKED the waiter, like it was a crime to be alone.

"Yes."

The waiter led Gray through into the restaurant, a brightly lit pizza place crammed with tables, just a short distance away from where Tom lived. "Is here okay?"

Gray's heart leapt when he caught sight of his son. He was facing his girlfriend, side on to Gray. Monica was very attractive and smiling broadly. She played with her dark hair while Tom talked. They clasped hands across the table. She appeared to be a little older than him.

"There, please." Gray pointed to a place a table away from Tom. The waiter led him over and Gray sat down. He was out of Tom's line of sight, but with a slight turn of his head, Gray could look at him without being obvious. Gray took a menu, and made a fast choice before sitting back and listening. He was desperate to go over, to pull out a chair and talk to him. But how would he introduce himself? What would he say? Gray had thought about this moment so often, yet now it was here his mind was a blank.

The restaurant was mainly empty so it was easy enough to eavesdrop onto Tom's conversation. The subjects they discussed were normal enough, about friends, about family, about work. Gray marvelled that Donna Massey had so readily given out information to a man she'd never met before. Northerners – too friendly.

As Gray's pizza arrived, an American, loaded with pepperoni and cheese, Monica pushed back her chair. She stood, her back arched as her posture adjusted for her pregnant belly. Gray was going to be a grandfather twice over. Monica slowly walked off, eyed by Tom the whole way.

This was Gray's moment. He could talk to Tom now. But he wasn't able to. It didn't feel right intrude on Tom's life like this, not now. He appeared happy and content. A new chapter about to start. Whatever Tom's memories were of Gray and his past they didn't matter. Only his future.

He caught the waiter's eye. "Could I get this to go, please? And the bill."

While Gray waited for his pizza to be boxed, he thought about what Hamson had said before he caught the train, when he'd tendered his resignation.

"I'll hold this until you get back, Sol." She'd put the letter into a drawer. "Just in case you change your mind."

THE END

If you enjoyed Bury The Bodies I'd greatly appreciate it if you would write a review. They really help authors like me grow and develop.

Thanks! It means a great deal to me.

And if you want to sign up to a periodic newsletter with information on launches, special offers etc. (no spam!) then you can do so HERE[1].

In return is a *free* book in the Konstantin series, ***Russian Roulette,*** a unique and gritty crime thriller featuring an ex-KGB operative living undercover in Margate. This is the blurb:

Konstantin Boryakov has just landed in England, a fugitive from the Russian authorities. He ends up in a run-down seaside town where trouble is always just round the corner.

Trouble has a habit of seeking out Konstantin Boryakov, whether he wants it or not. Starting from the moment he arrives in the seedy seaside town of Margate where he's supposed to be in hiding from his Russian ex-employers. Konstantin has to overcome the drug dealer, the loan shark and Fat Gary, all round idiot. Then there's the so-called good guys, the councillors and lawyers who are worse than the criminals.

All Konstantin wants is to be left alone. But it's not to be. Enter Fidelity Brown, aka Plastic Fantastic, the dildo wielding dominatrix who has her own mélange of secrets and lies, and nightclub owner Ken who's connected to all the wrong people.

---

1. https://mailchi.mp/4bbaf7efe867/keith-nixon-free-book

Both help the Russian with the heap of problems delivered to his doorstep.

Cue deception, murder, mayhem as Konstantin settles into his new life. Margate will never be the same again. And neither will Konstantin...

Meet Konstantin Boryakov, the enigmatic ex-KGB agent and tramp with a dark history and darker future in the start of a unique crime thriller series. Pick up *Russian Roulette* to find out what all the fuss is about.

Other Novels By Keith Nixon

The Solomon Gray Series
Dig Two Graves
Burn The Evidence
Beg For Mercy
Bury The Bodies
The Konstantin Series
Russian Roulette
The Fix
I'm Dead Again
Dark Heart, Heavy Soul
The DI Granger Series
The Corpse Role
The Caradoc Series
The Eagle's Shadow
The Eagle's Blood

Acknowledgements

Any novel (or *series* of novels in this case) is the work of multiple people and this is entirely true here. Gray's first outing, *Dig Two Graves* as it became, started life as a Nanowrimo entry back in November 2008. The original draft was, frankly, awful and it ended up in the sock drawer.

I came across it again in 2015 when I was between books and trying to figure out what to write next. I picked the manuscript up and read it on a train back from London for some reason I felt the contents (despite the aforementioned messy attributes) had some merit. To cut a very long story short, there followed a multitude of rewrites and several title changes until finally it was picked up by Bastei Luebbe in October 2017. It's been quite a process.

First and foremost, my immense thanks go to my editor and mentor, Allan Guthrie. Sir, you are a superstar.

And Lori Herber, who put up with a torrent of emails from me of varying levels of stupidity and provided much valuable critical assessment of the manuscripts. Special mention also to Kerstin Fricke for translation and I couldn't forget Eleanor Abraham whose attention to detail is second to none.

There were also a number of other people who helped kick the book into shape well before publication. Julie Lewthwaite, Christina Philippou and Liz Barnsley, take a bow. And to legal eagle Neil Wright for his procedural advice.

And thanks to fellow authors who provided blurbs and supported the process along the way – Tim Baker, Ken Bruen, Mike Craven, Mason Cross, Ed James, Howard Linskey and Luca Veste. Also my indie colleagues in the background – Linda Acaster, Jason Beech, Nigel Bird, Paul Brazill, Gordon Brown, Sherv Jamali, Rob Johnson, Martin Stanley and Mark Wilson.

Last, but certainly not least, are the multitude of bloggers, readers and reviewers – there's simply too many to name and I'd hate to miss anyone out (you know who you are). However, several of the hard-working admin team at THE Book Club, founded by Tracy Fenton, merit mention for bringing Solomon Gray to a much wider audience – Helen Boyce and Melanie Preston Lewis. Along with Sandra Mangan and Garrick Webster at Crime Fiction Lover and Al Kunz and Linda McKinney at Big Al's Books and Pals.

Thanks one and all. I owe you a beer.

About The Author

Keith Nixon is a British born writer of crime and historical fiction novels. Originally, he trained as a chemist, but Keith is now in a senior sales role for a high-tech business. Keith currently lives with his family in the North West of England.

Readers can connect with Keith on various social media platforms:

Web: http://www.keithnixon.co.uk
Twitter: @knntom[1]
Facebook: Keithnixonauthor[2]
Blog: www.keithnixon.co.uk/blog[3]

---

1. https://twitter.com/knntom
2. https://www.facebook.com/keithnixonauthor/
3. http://www.keithnixon.co.uk/blog

Bury The Bodies
Published by Gladius Press 2018
Copyright © Keith Nixon 2018
First Edition

Keith Nixon has asserted his right under the Copyright, Designs and Patents Act 1998 to be identified as the author of this work

CONDITIONS OF SALE

All rights reserved. No part of this publication may be reproduced, stored in a retrieval system, or transmitted in any form or by any means, electronic, mechanical, photocopying, scanning, recording or otherwise, without the prior permission of the publisher

This book has been sold subject to the condition that it shall not, by way of trade or otherwise, be lent, resold, hired out, or otherwise circulated without the publisher's prior consent in any form of binding or cover other than that in which it is published and without a similar condition including this condition being imposed on the subsequent purchaser.

All characters in this publication are fictitious and any resemblance to real persons, living or dead is purely coincidental.

Cover design by Jim Divine.

Don't miss out!

Visit the website below and you can sign up to receive emails whenever Keith Nixon publishes a new book. There's no charge and no obligation.

https://books2read.com/r/B-A-BGNH-WBXW

BOOKS 2 READ

Connecting independent readers to independent writers.

Did you love *Bury The Bodies*? Then you should read *Russian Roulette* by Keith Nixon!

A reluctant investigator, a seedy English seaside Town, a criminal underbelly.

Trouble has a habit of seeking out Konstantin, whether he wants it or not. Starting from the moment he arrives in the seedy seaside town of Margate where he's supposed to be in hiding from his ex-employers. Konstantin has to overcome the drug dealer, the loan shark and a Liverpudlian gangster. Then there's the so-called good guys, the councilors and lawyers who are worse than the criminals.

All Konstantin wants is to be left alone. But it's not to be. Enter Fidelity Brown, aka Plastic Fantastic, a dominatrix who has her own mélange of secrets and lies, and nightclub owner Ken who's connected to all the wrong people. Both help Konstantin solve the cases dropped on his doorstep.

Cue deception, murder, mayhem as the Russian settles into his new life. Margate will never be the same again. And neither will Konstantin...

Meet the enigmatic Konstantin, a man with a dark history and darker future in the start of a unique crime thriller series laced with a healthy dose of black humour. Pick up Russian Roulette to find out what all the fuss is about.

What Readers Say

'An ex-convict Russian spy who I absolutely adore and want to invite over for dinner!' 'Gritty and glorious, dirty and dynamic, fast and furious.' 'I can't wait to start the next book and see what else is on store for Konstantin.' 'Top notch entertainment from Keith Nixon.' 'I adored Konstantin, although I'm not sure I was supposed to!' 'If you liked LA Confidential, you'll love this.' 'I can't recommend this book enough.'

What Others Say

'Criminally underrated.' **MW Craven**, author of *The Washington Poe series* 'One hell of a writer.' **Ken Bruen**, Author of *The Jack Taylor series* 'I have to liken reading this novel to being a smoker - it leaves a dirty taste in your mouth but you JUST CAN'T STOP.' **Lisa Hall**, author of *Between You and Me, Tell Me No Lies, The Party* 'Nixon writes hard-hitting fiction, with a dash of humour, a cast of great characters, and a dollop of violence. Konstantin is a fantastic creation.' **Luca Veste**, author of *The Murphy and Rossi series* and *The Bonekeeper* 'This is a brilliant, fun book. Violent, yes. Dark, yes. But it has black humour running all the way through it. And it made me want to visit Margate. I loved it and was delighted to see there are other books featuring Konstantin and look forward to reading more of his adventures.' **Suze Reviews** 'Gritty and glorious, dirty and dynamic, fast and furious. My kind of book.' **Col's Criminal Library** 'A superior action-thriller, layered with flashbacks, intriguing characters and tendon-snapping sequences of graphic violence.' **Murder, Mayhem and More** 'A fast-paced and witty tale.' **Big Al's Books and Pals** 'With his unique style of writing, the author grabs the reader's attention and makes for an entertaining read.' **By The Letter Book Reviews** 'Tight, punchy with a distinct voice.' **Crimesquad**

Also by Keith Nixon

Caradoc
The Eagle's Shadow

Detective Solomon Gray
Dig Two Graves
Burn The Evidence
Beg For Mercy
Bury The Bodies

DI Granger
The Corpse Role

Konstantin
Russian Roulette
The Fix
I'm Dead Again

Dark Heart, Heavy Soul

Standalone
The Solomon Gray Series: Books 1 to 4: Gripping Police Thrillers With A Difference

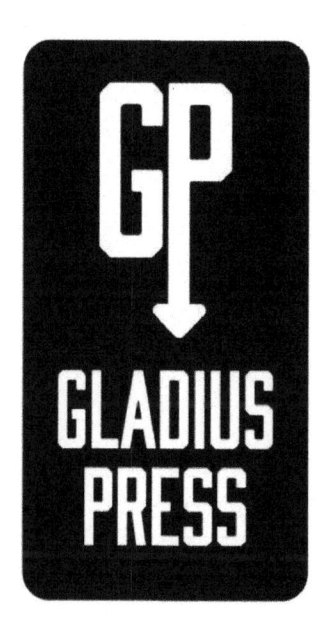

About the Publisher

Gladius Press is a small, yet highly innovative publisher of crime, humour and historical fiction novels based in Manchester in the UK.

Printed in Great Britain
by Amazon